THE
BEAR

Raymond Briggs

KU-317-414

Red Fox

A Red Fox Book

Published by Random House Children's Books
20 Vauxhall Bridge Road, London SW1V 2SA

A division of Random House UK Ltd
London Melbourne Sydney Auckland
Johannesburg and agencies throughout the world

Copyright © 1994 Raymond Briggs

1 3 5 7 9 10 8 6 4 2

First published in Great Britain by
Julia MacRae 1994

Red Fox edition 1996

This book is sold subject to the condition that it shall not,
by way of trade or otherwise, be lent, resold, hired out, or
otherwise circulated without the publisher's prior consent in
any form of binding or cover other than that in which it is
published and without a similar condition including this
condition being imposed on the subsequent purchaser.

The right of Raymond Briggs to be identified as the author
and illustrator of this work has been asserted by him in
accordance with the Copyright, Designs and Patents Act, 1988.

Printed in Hong Kong

RANDOM HOUSE UK Limited Reg. No. 954009

ISBN 0 09 938561 9

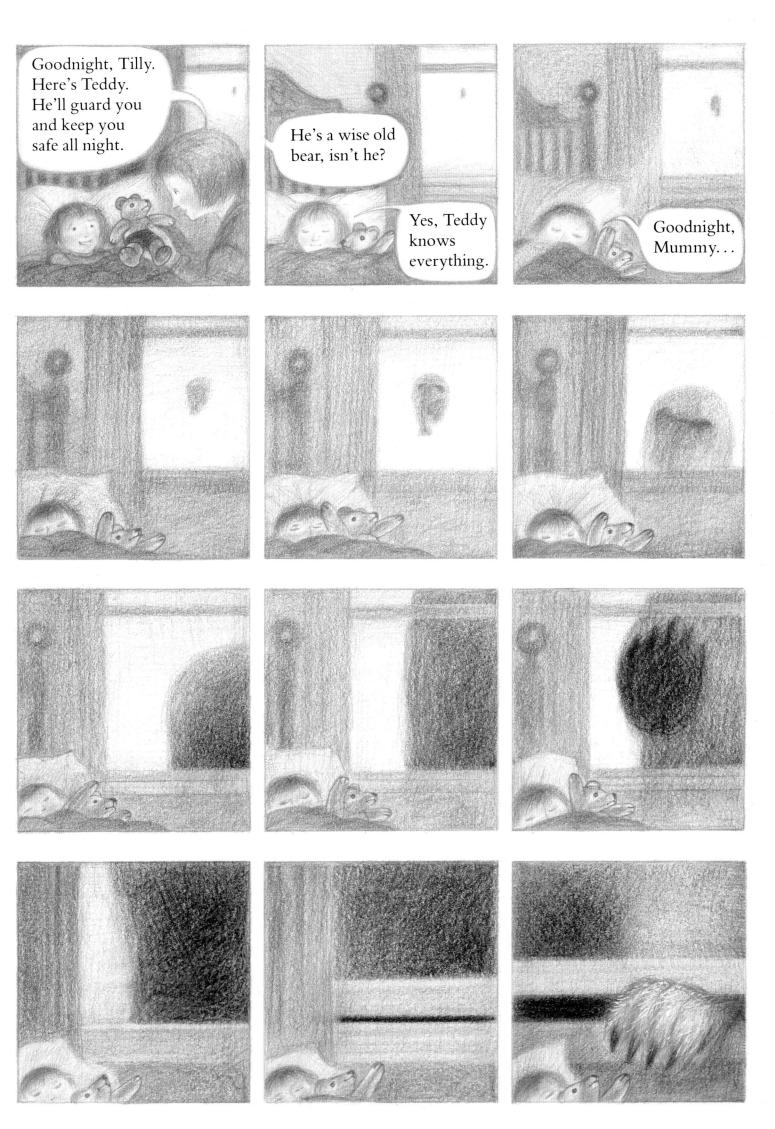

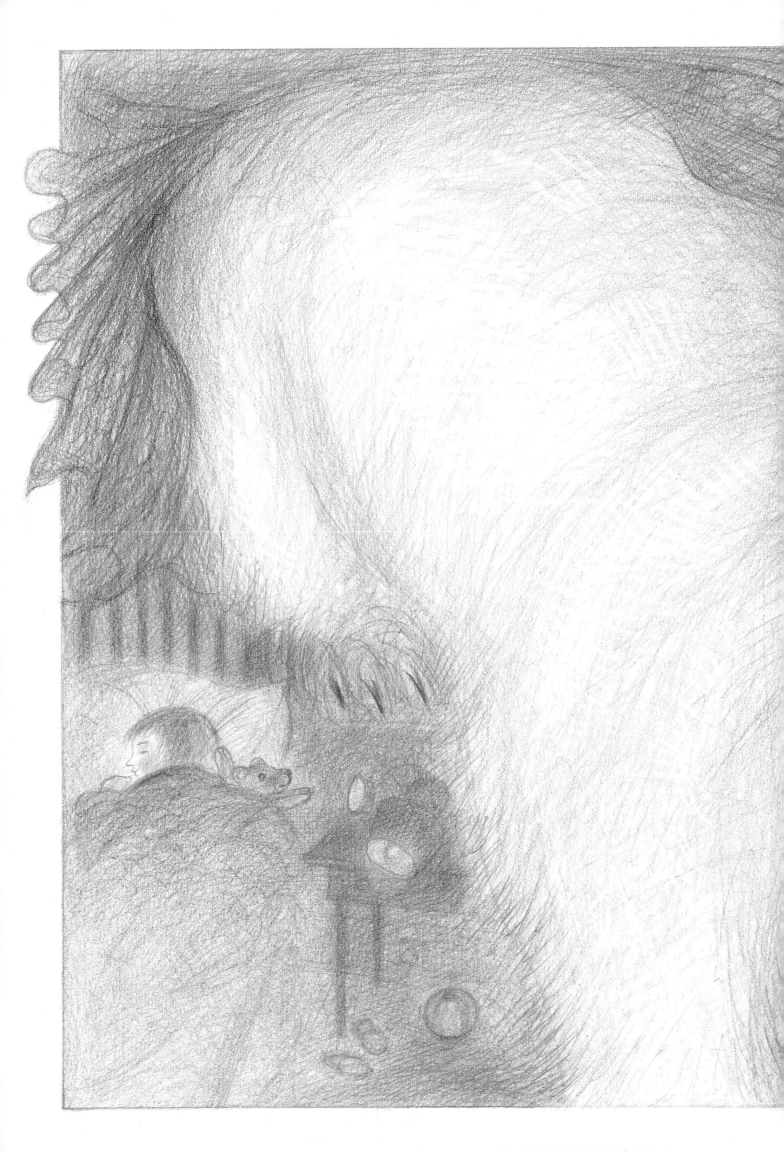

Mmmm . . .

Oh, hello.

It's a bear.

Hello, Bear.

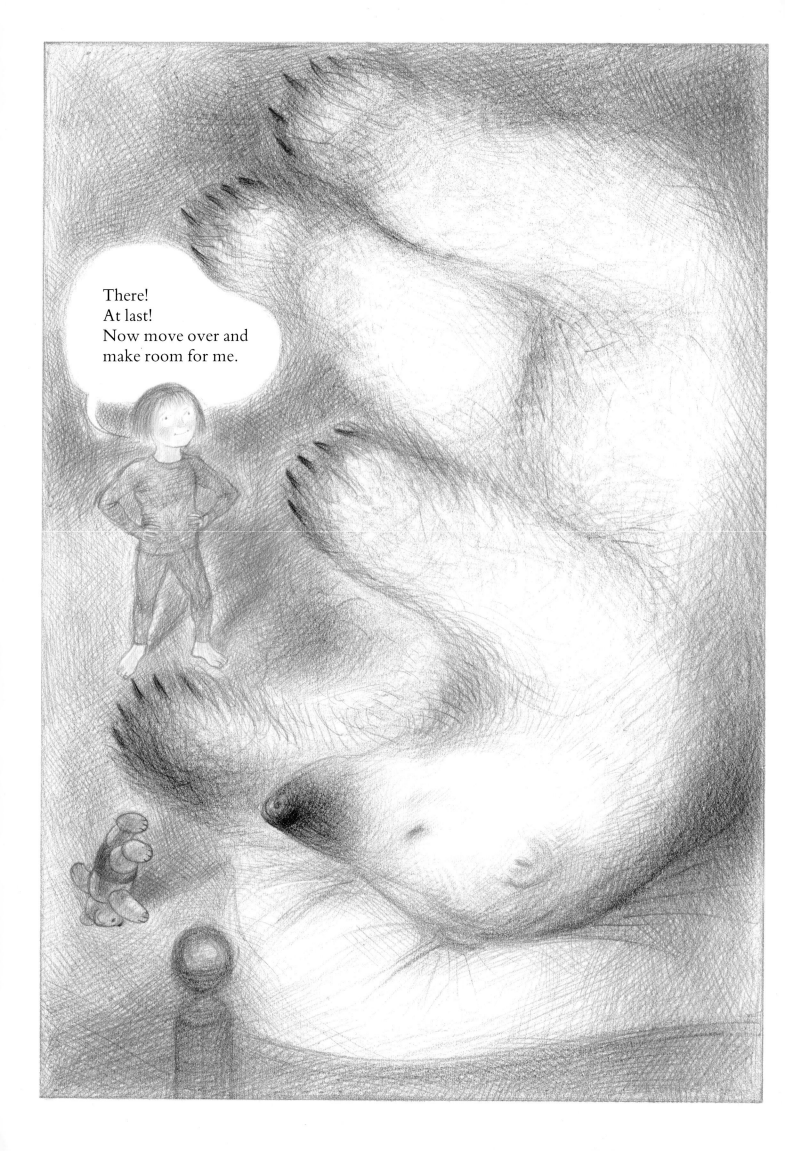

Mummy! Mummy! Daddy!
I was woken up by a bear!

Oh? What a surprise.
Was he a nice bear?

He licked my face with his tongue to wake me up.

Did he?

It was ever so rough.
And he had great big black wet nostrils
blowing hot air in my face.

Tilly! That's not very nice.

It's true!
He wanted to be friendly.

Well, mind you're friendly back.

You should see his teeth!
They're all yellow and enormous.
Longer than my fingers.
He's got real fangs.
I saw them when he yawned.
And his claws!
They're all black and curved like hooks.
He could easily tear me to bits
and eat me.

Tilly!
For goodness' sake!

He wouldn't though.
He really likes me. I can tell.

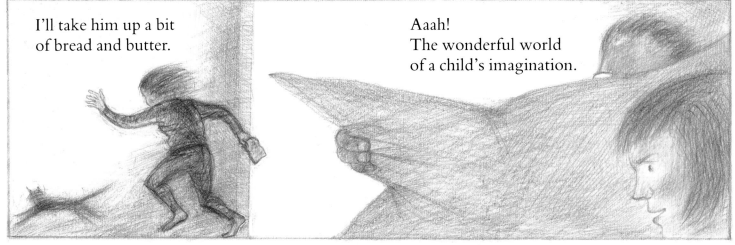

I'll take him up a bit
of bread and butter.

Aaah!
The wonderful world
of a child's imagination.

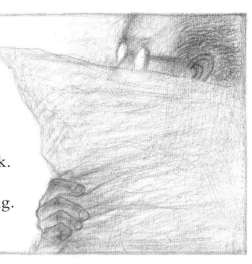

He's asleep now.
I've covered him up
with my duvet.

Did he like the bread
and butter?

He just licked it up with one flick.
You should see his tongue!
It's all black and about a foot long.

Ugh! Tilly!

Can he stay, Mummy?

Stay?
Yes, of course.
He can have
the spare bedroom.

No, I want him to sleep
with me.

Won't he roll over and squash
you in the night?

No, he'll just cuddle me.
I won't need a duvet.
He's the cuddliest thing
in the whole world.

Oh?
What about me?

You've got no *fur*, Daddy.
But you're *quite* nice.
I do still like you a *little* bit.

Oh, good.
I know I can't compete
with a bear.

Now you will be all right, won't you, Tilly?

Yes, Mummy.

Daddy is in his workshop,
but try not to bother him too often.

Yes, Mummy.
Don't fuss.
I've got the bear to guard me.

Yes, of course.
I really must dash.

Can I get extra milk from the milkman,
for the bear?

What?
Oh yes, of course.
Get as much as you like.
Byebye, Tilly.
Be good.

Byebye, Mummy.

You will make your bed, won't you?

I can't.
The bear is still in it.

Oh yes, well –
Never mind then –
Bye!

Hello, young lady.

Hello.
Can I have some extra
milk, please?
I've got a bear staying.

A bear, eh?
You'll need a lot
of extra milk
for a bear.
Is it a big bear?

Enormous.

Well . . .
Twenty pints, then?

I think one extra
will be sufficient,
thank you.

Bear!
Bear!
Where are you?

Oh no! Don't!
Come away.

Look, here's
some water.

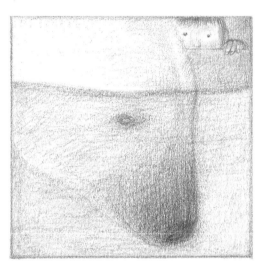

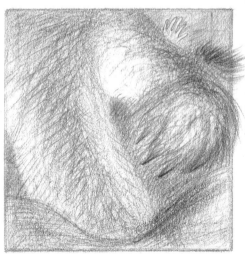

Now look what you've done. I'm all wet.

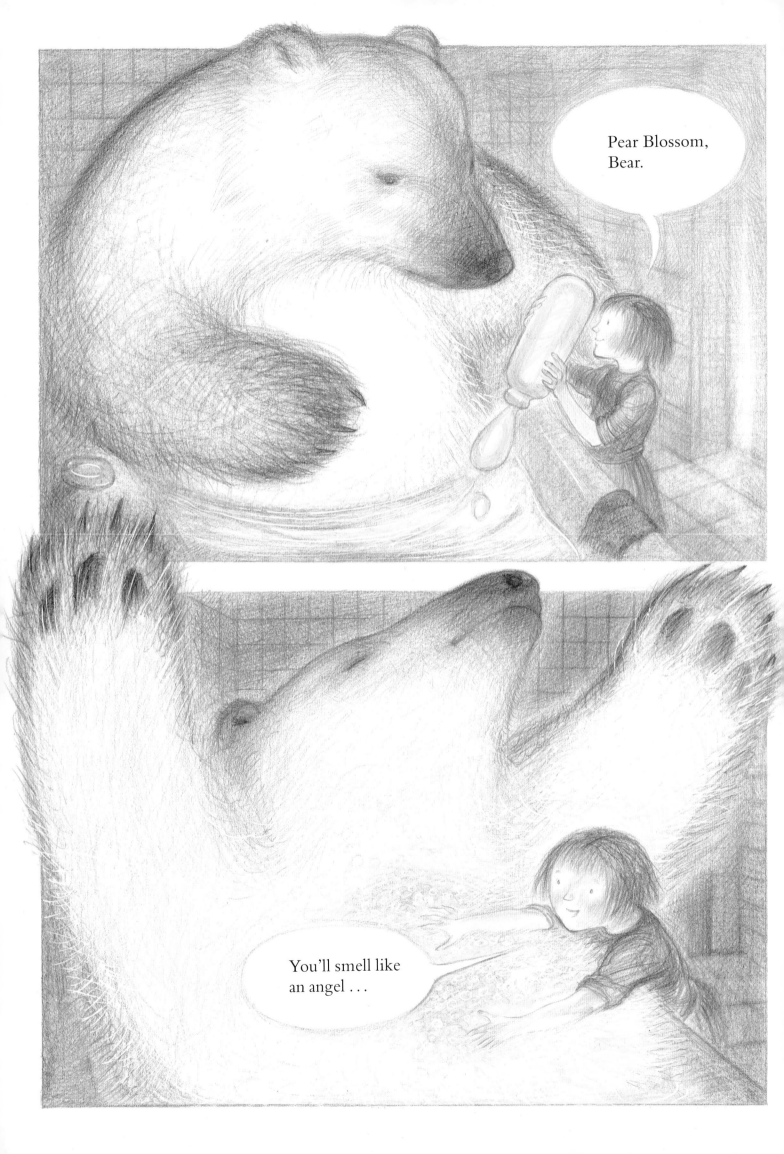

You silly bear. You've soaked me *again*.

I'll dry us in the kitchen.

You do cause a lot of work, Bear.

Is it true bears like honey?
Try some.
It's Daddy's very own.

My!
You are quick.
It's all gone.
You are a greedy pig, Bear.

Bear! Bear!

Where are you?

How can you disappear when you're so big?

OH NO!

What are you up to, Tilly?

The bear's done a poo. I'm burying it.

Oh, I see. Good girl.

Oh, there you are at last.
You're a very naughty bear,
making messes.

BAD
BOY!

DON'T!

Now I've got to go
and wash again.
Don't disappear.
Wait here.

Oh, you BEAST!
You've weed on the floor!

Horrible! Horrible!
Horrible!

You are *awful*!
I *hate* you.
Don't you dare do it again.

I'm going upstairs to have
a long think about what to do
with you, Bear. So wait here.

Look, Bear, I've decided you and
I have got to have a serious talk.
Come and sit down properly.

Now listen.
You know Mummy said you could have
the spare bedroom?
Well, she's never once seen you
and she may change her mind when
she finds out how big you are.
And if you are going to do poos and wees
all over the house, she'll *never* let you stay.
Mummy and Daddy mustn't see you
or they might put you out.
Do you understand?

Will you pay attention
when I'm talking to you!

Oh, you're *hopeless*!
You're always yawning
and falling asleep.

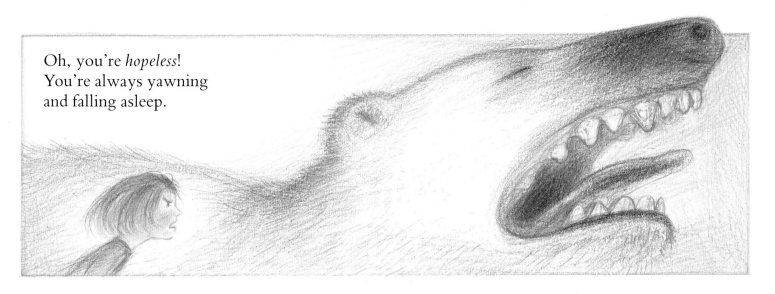

WAKE UP!
WAKE UP!

Come with me, Bear.

I'm going to put you
in the spare bedroom.

No! *Left* here, stupid.

Up the stairs
you go.
Giddy up!

Now, you can *hide* in there,
but remember you're going to sleep with me.

NO!
Not in here!
It's Mummy
and Daddy's
bedroom.

Bear! Bear!
You can't hide *there*!

Oh, you silly bear!
You'll get such
a ticking off!

Hello, Tilly!
Like something to eat?

Yes, please, I'm starving.
The bear is a lot of work, Daddy.

Is he settling in?

Yes, he's fast asleep in your bed.

Oh, good.
Will he sleep in between me and Mummy?

No. He's going to sleep with me.
You mustn't go in, you'll wake him up.

All right.
I'll go about on tiptoe
and we'll talk in whispers.

Hello,
Tilly!

Mummy!

Have you been all right?
Has the bear been looking
after you?

Sssh!

What?

Sssh! He's asleep.
In our bed.

Who is?

The bear. Sssh!
Mustn't go in
our bedroom.
Sssh!

Oh, I see.
Sssh!
We must whisper.

Yes, Sssh!

He's so big and quiet, Mummy.
He's the silentest thing I've ever known.
He's like a great big white ghost.

 Is he? He sounds like
 a polar bear.

I can't even hear him breathing
except when he cuddles me.
Then I can hear his heart beating,
too. His heart goes ever so slow –
it goes BOOM… ages ages ages
BOOM… ages ages ages BOOM,
like that.

 Well, I never. He's a long way
 from home, isn't he?

No, he's going to live here with me.
His fur is terrifically thick and
when I bury my nose in it,
it's ever so smelly, too.

 Oh Tilly, really!

No, it's a lovely smell.
All dark and smoky.

The bear is very good at hiding, Daddy.
Sometimes I look all over the house
and I can't find him.

But you say he is enormous?

He is, but he just seems to vanish like magic.
He could be in this room now
and you'd never know.

Golly!
Just imagine a great
big bear in here now!
I feel quite frightened.

Goodnight, darling.

Goodnight, Mummy.

Goodnight, Teddy.

There!

Now Tilly, whatever have you been
up to in our bedroom?

Oh, that wasn't me, Mummy.
That was the bear.

Well, the bear should have
tidied up, then.

I did tick him off.
I expect that's why he's hiding
under the bed. He's sulking.

Is he there now?

Yes, of course he is.

Shall I give him a
goodnight kiss, too?

No, better not.
I think he's asleep.

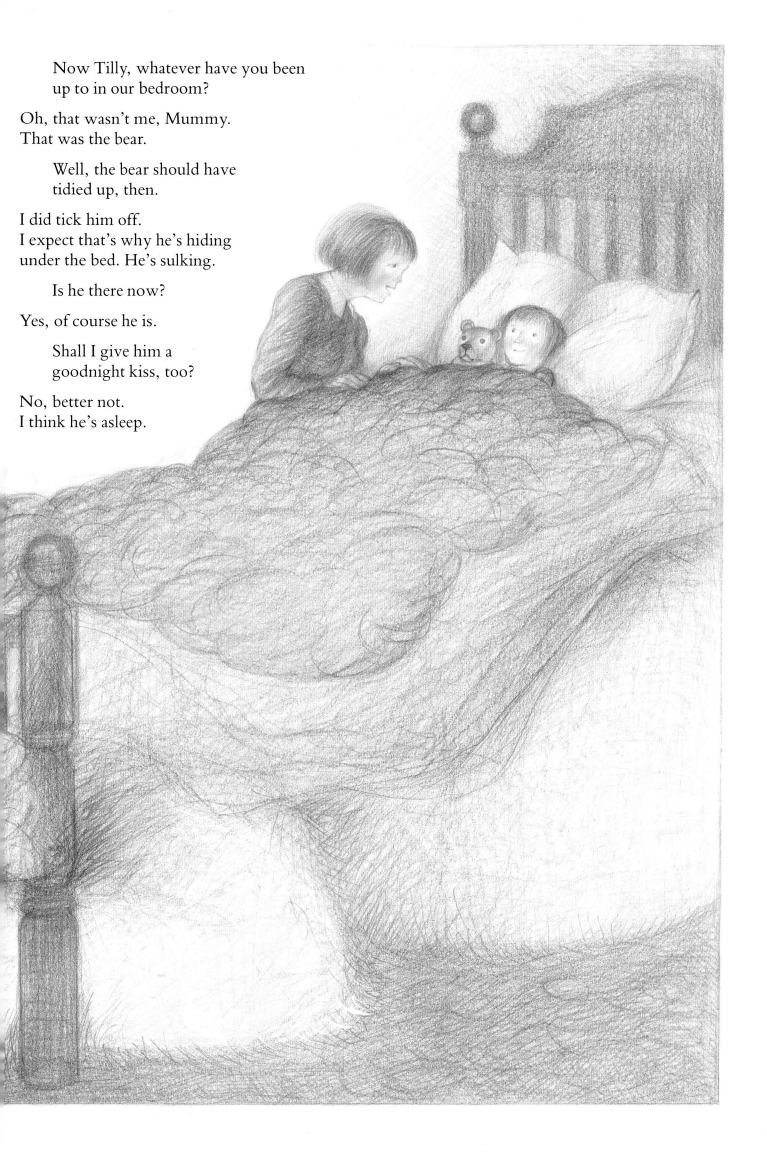

Come on, Bear. Mummy's gone.
You can come to bed now.

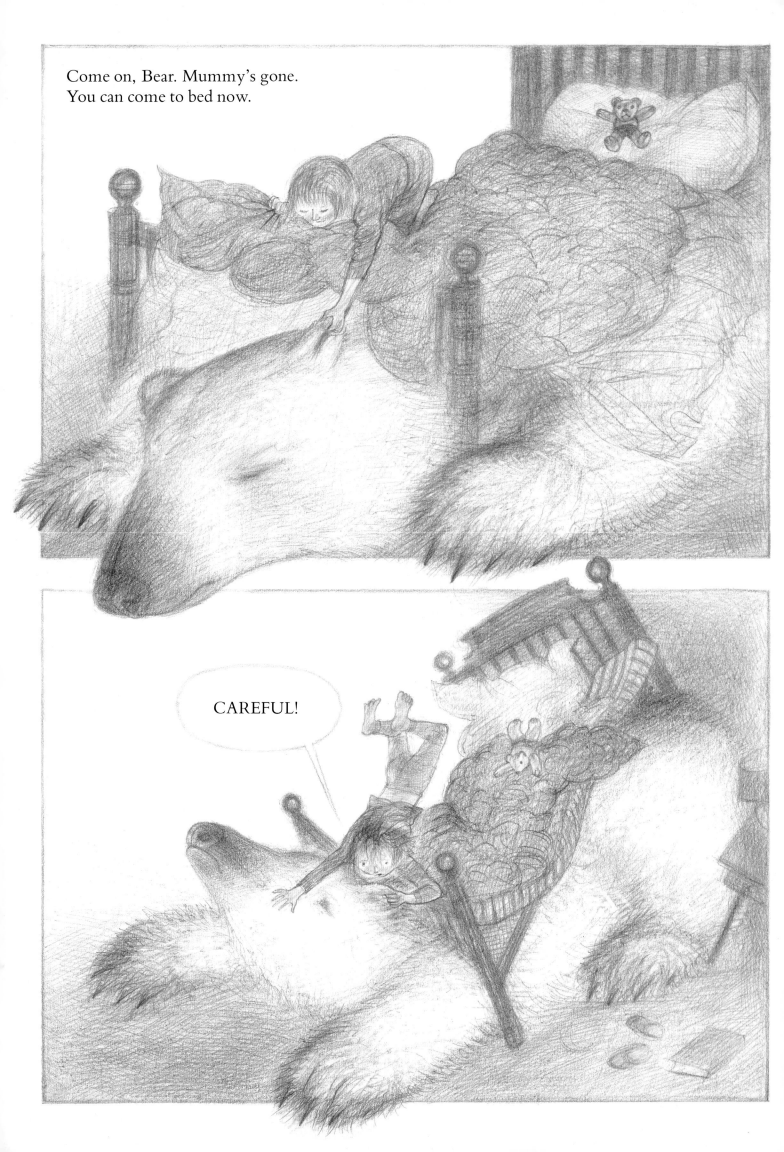

CAREFUL!

I love you,
Bear,

with all
my heart . . .

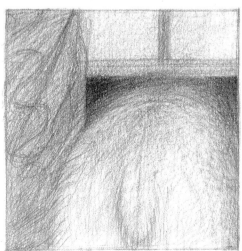

Tilly! Whatever's the matter?

He's gone!
He's gone!

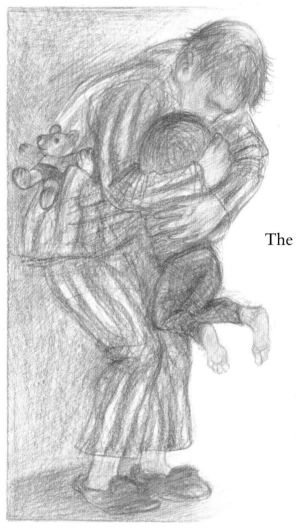

Who?

The bear! He's gone!

Never mind, Tilly, sweetheart.
Don't cry, darling.
Bears can't live in houses
with people, can they, Teddy?
That sort of thing only
happens in story books.
Look Tilly, Teddy's nodding.
And he knows all
about bears,
don't you, Teddy?

Yes.
Teddy knows
everything.

KU-465-742

OXFORD INTENSIVE ENGLISH COURSES

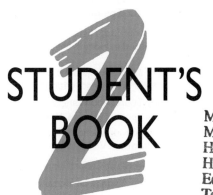

STUDENT'S
BOOK

Moray House English Language Centre
Moray House Institute of Education
Heriot-Watt University
Holyrood Road
Edinburgh EH8 8AQ
Tel: 0131 558 6332   Fax: 0131 557 5138

DAVID BOLTON
CLIVE OXENDEN
LEN PETERSON

Oxford University Press

Oxford University Press
Walton Street, Oxford OX2 6DP

Oxford New York
Athens Auckland Bangkok Bombay
Calcutta Cape Town Dar es Salaam Delhi
Florence Hong Kong Istanbul Karachi
Kuala Lumpur Madras Madrid Melbourne
Mexico City Nairobi Paris Singapore
Taipei Tokyo Toronto

and associated companies in
Berlin Ibadan

OXFORD and OXFORD ENGLISH are trade marks of
Oxford University Press

ISBN 0 19 432357 9

© Oxford University Press 1989

First published 1989
Fifth impression 1995

No unauthorized photocopying

All rights reserved. No part of this publication may be
reproduced, stored in a retrieval system, or transmitted, in
any form or by any means, electronic, mechanical,
photocopying, recording or otherwise, without the prior
written permission of Oxford University Press.

This book is sold subject to the condition that it shall not, by
way of trade or otherwise, be lent, re-sold, hired out, or
otherwise circulated without the publisher's prior consent in
any form of binding or cover other than that in which it is
published and without a similar condition including this
condition being imposed on the subsequent purchaser.

Typeset by Pentacor Ltd, High Wycombe, Bucks
Printed in Hong Kong

The authors would like to acknowledge the help and cooperation of
the following schools in the production of this course:

Anglo European Study Tours, Abon Language School, Bristol;
Centro Europeo de Idiomas, Valencia;

IHSP, Bromley; ITS Hastings; King's School, Beckenham; The British
Institute, Valencia

and the following people at Oxford University Press:

Alison Findlay, Coralie Green, Yvonne de Henseler, Jean Hindmarch,
Claire Nicholl, Rosy Nixon, James Richardson, Greg Sweetnam,
Andy Younger.

Special thanks also go to Paul Power, Fiona Wright and Simon Taylor.

The publishers would like to thank the following for their permission
to reproduce photographs:

Anthony Blake, Britain on View Photographic Library, Brittany Ferries,
Colorific, Ronald Grant Archive, Sally & Richard Greenhill, Rex
Features Ltd, Supersport, Elizabeth Whiting Exteriors

and the following for their time and assistance:

British Rail, Oxford; Lake School of English, Oxford; London
Transport; Omni Jeans, Oxford; Temple Cowley Swimming Pool,
Oxford; Walton Street Post Office, Oxford; Wychwood School;
Oxford.

Location and studio photography by:

Catherine Blackie, Rob Judges, Mark Mason, Garry & Marilyn O'Brien.

Illustrations by:

Jacqueline Bissett, Kate Charlesworth, Susannah English, Sian Leetham,
Maggie Ling, Andrew MacConville, Mohsen John Modaberi, Bill Piggins,
Kim Raymond, Christine Roche, Nick Sharratt, Paul Thomas.

CONTENTS

UNIT	LESSON 1	LESSON 2	LESSON 3
	GRAMMAR IN ACTION	ENGLISH IN SITUATIONS	FUN WITH ENGLISH
1 PAGES 6–11	*to be* – present tense *have got* *can/can't* present simple (including *do* construction)	introductions greetings asking for things asking to borrow things saying goodbye	*Further practice in:* pronunciation listening vocabulary reading speaking finding out about the UK
2 PAGES 12–17	present simple/present continuous contrasted imperatives demonstratives	using English money asking about the price of things asking about and telling the time	*Further practice in:* pronunciation listening vocabulary reading speaking finding out about the UK
3 PAGES 18–23	*there is/there are* *much/many/a lot of* countable/uncountable nouns	asking about and describing where buildings/places are accepting and refusing food at mealtimes	*Further practice in:* pronunciation listening vocabulary reading speaking finding out about the UK
4 PAGES 24–29	past simple *there was/there were* infinitive of purpose *some/any*	spelling in English apologizing/responding to apologies	*Further practice in:* pronunciation listening vocabulary reading speaking finding out about the UK
5 PAGES 30–35	past simple adverbs of frequency comparatives	using a payphone and making an international phone call cashing traveller's cheques changing money talking about days and dates	*Further practice in:* pronunciation listening vocabulary reading speaking finding out about the UK
6 PAGES 36–41	future *going to* present continuous for future *like (hate, enjoy) + ing* form	buying clothes talking about sizes and colours	*Further practice in:* pronunciation listening vocabulary reading speaking finding out about the UK

UNIT	LESSON 1	LESSON 2	LESSON 3
	GRAMMAR IN ACTION	**ENGLISH IN SITUATIONS**	**FUN WITH ENGLISH**
7 PAGES 42–47	*will* in first conditional superlatives	using the telephone telephone numbers taking messages on the telephone	*Further practice in:* pronunciation listening vocabulary reading speaking finding out about the UK
8 PAGES 48–53	present perfect with *yet*/ *already*/*ever*/*never*/*just* + indefinite time	using public transport	*Further practice in:* pronunciation listening vocabulary reading speaking finding out about the UK
9 PAGES 54–59	present perfect with *for*/ *since* present perfect/past simple contrast relative pronouns *who*/ *which*	asking permission inviting and making offers accepting/refusing invitations and offers apologizing and making excuses	*Further practice in:* pronunciation listening vocabulary reading speaking finding out about the UK
10 PAGES 60–65	past continuous/past simple contrasted adverbs of manner	talking about parts of the body asking/saying what's the matter at the doctor's	*Further practice in:* pronunciation listening vocabulary reading speaking finding out about the UK
11 PAGES 66–71	passives—present/past	talking about rules and obligations	*Further practice in:* pronunciation listening vocabulary reading speaking finding out about the UK
12 PAGES 72–77	revision	saying goodbye thanking revision	*Further practice in:* pronunciation listening vocabulary reading speaking finding out about the UK

UNIT ONE · LESSON ONE

The welcome party

1 Questions and answers

a Match the questions on the left with the answers on the right.

Example: 2 – f

1 Are you English?	a) Yes, please.
2 Can you speak French?	b) Yes, I do.
3 Is your English very good?	c) No, I'm not.
4 Do you want a drink?	d) No, it isn't.
5 Have you got a watch?	e) Switzerland.
6 What's the time, please?	f) Yes, a bit.
7 Do you like pop music?	g) Yes, I can.
8 Where are you from?	h) I don't know.
9 Can you dance?	i) No, I haven't.

b Work in pairs. Ask and answer the questions with true answers.

2 Find out

a What questions must you ask to fill in the table below?

Examples:
What's your name?
How old are you?

	Student A	Student B	Student C
Name			
Age			
Town / City			
Language (s)			
Hobbies			

b Move round the class and ask three students the questions. Fill in the table.

c Tell the class about *one* of the students you spoke to.

Example:
This is Luisa. She's 16. She's from Valencia in Spain. She speaks Spanish, French and English. She likes windsurfing.

3 About yourself

a Complete these sentences about yourself on a piece of paper.

I can . . .   but I can't . . .
I like . . .   but I don't like . . .
I've got . . .   but I haven't got . . .

b Fold the piece of paper and put it into a hat or bag. Take out a different piece of paper. Tell the rest of the class about the student who wrote the sentences on it.

Example:
X can windsurf but he / she can't ride a horse.
X likes pizzas but doesn't like spaghetti.
X has got a cassette player but he / she hasn't got a camera.

The rest of the class guess who X is.

4 Find partners

a Divide the class into two halves. (If possible all the boys are in one half and all the girls in the other.)
The two halves stand at opposite sides of the room.

b Meet in the middle of the room and ask each other questions to find:

	Names
• a person whose surname ends with the same letter as yours	
• a person whose birthday is in the same month as yours	
• a person who's got the same number of brothers as you	
• a person who's got the same number of sisters as you	
• a person whose telephone number begins with the same figure as yours	
• a person who likes the same pop group / singer as you.	

c The student with the most names is the winner.

Grammar summary: page 82

7

I 🖾 Introductions

Hi. I'm Martin.

Hello. My name's Christina.

Um . . . Martin, this is Hannah.

Hi Anna. Nice to meet you.

No, not Anna—Hannah.

Oh, I'm sorry. H—H—Hannah!!

a Practise the dialogue in groups of three using the same names.

b Form different groups of three. Practise the dialogue again but use your own names. One of you must always make a mistake with a name.

Note: You may hear adults say, 'How do you do?' The answer is, 'How do you do?'

How do you do? I'm Sarah Young.

How do you do? My name's Richard Ellis.

2 🖾 Greetings

a Practise the dialogue in pairs using your own names. Change roles.

b Move around the class. Greet at least three different students. Change the underlined phrases to:

How are things?   *All right, thanks.*
How's it going?   *Not too bad, thanks.*

c Do the same again without looking in your book but using all the different phrases.

Hello Nicky. How are you?

Fine, thanks. And you?

OK thanks.

3 Asking for things

| Can Could | I have . . . , please? | Yes, here you are. Yes, of course. |

a Work in pairs. Ask each other for the things in the pictures.

Example:
A *Can I have a 20p stamp, please?*
B *Yes, here you are.*

b Now think of other things to ask each other for in the same way.

4 What do they want?

🎧 Listen to the cassette. Tick the things which each person asks for.

1 coffee ☐   tea ☐
   black ☐   white ☐

2 biscuits ☐   crisps ☐
   plain ☐   salt & vinegar ☐   cheese & onion ☐

3 Napolitana ☐   Margarita ☐   vegetarian ☐
   small ☐   medium ☐   large ☐

4 strawberry ☐   vanilla ☐   chocolate ☐
   large ☐   medium ☐   small ☐

5 Asking to borrow things

Can	I borrow . . . please?	Yes, of course.
Could		Yes, here you are.
		No, I'm afraid not.
		No, I'm sorry (you can't).

a Work in pairs. Student A asks to borrow the things in the pictures, student B answers.

Example:
A *Can I borrow your dictionary, please?*
B *Yes, of course.*

A *Could I borrow £5, please?*
B *No, I'm afraid not. (I haven't got £5.)*

b Go round the class asking to borrow different things from other students as above.

6 🎧 Saying goodbye

Boy *I must go now. Bye.*
Girl *Cheerio.*

(pause)

Girl *Are you still there?*
Boy *Yes, are you?*
Girl *Yes.*

(pause)

This is silly. See you tomorrow. Goodbye.
Boy *Yes, see you. Bye.*
Girl *Bye bye.*

(long pause)

Girl *Hello . . . ?*

a Practise the dialogue in pairs. Change roles.

b Go round the class saying goodbye to other students. Use the words and phrases below.

Goodbye. See you	later.
Bye.	tomorrow.
Bye bye.	soon.
Cheerio.	on (Saturday).

Summary of English in situations

- introducing yourself and other people
- greeting people
- asking for things
- asking to borrow things
- saying goodbye

1 Sound right

a Find pairs of words which rhyme.

Example: *two – do*

two	hot
what	your
try	know
here	he's
for	**do**
go	aren't
good	eye
are	near
please	could
can't	bar

b Form two teams. The teacher writes words from the two lists on the blackboard. The teams take it in turn to add words to the lists. The words must rhyme but you must not write words from the other team's list. The team with the longest list is the winner.

c Listen and repeat the rhyming words on the board.

d Practise pronouncing the words again without listening first.

2 Listen to this

Listen to several people talking at a party. Write the missing responses in the empty speech bubbles.

What language do you speak?

Where are you from?

Hello. My name's Richard.

How do you do?

Are you English?

Do you smoke?

I must go now. Goodbye.

Hello. How are you?

Do you want a drink?

I'm very sorry.

3 Work on words

a Which word in each group does *not* go with the other three?

Example: black

white

(large)

pink

1 dictionary
A newspaper
B magazine
C word

2 Switzerland
German
French
Italian

3 goodbye
cheerio
hi
bye

4 music
dance
listen
play

5 OK
all right
fine
terrible

6 eye
ear
face
mouth

7 hello
hi
good morning
cheerio

8 packet
can
bottle
cup

9 vanilla
strawberry
chocolate
vegetarian

10 tomato
mushroom
cheese
onion

11 salt
pepper
vinegar
plain

12 hot
cold
warm
temperature

b Explain why 'the odd word out' does not go with the other three.

Example:
'large' does not go with black, white, or pink because they are all colours while 'large' describes the size of something or somebody.

c Find a fourth word which goes with the other three.

Example:
black   white   pink   *blue*

4 Play games in English

Twenty questions

One student at a time thinks of an object or thing in the room.

Other students in the class try to guess what it is by asking questions.

Examples:
Can you see it?
Is it big / small?
Can you wear it?
Have you got one?
Is it made of wood?
Is it very heavy?
Can you write with it?
Is it expensive?
Is there only one in the room?

The student who is answering can only give Yes / No answers.

Examples:
Yes, I can.
No, it isn't.
No, I haven't.
Yes, it is.

5 Read and think

Who's who?

Read the following information. Decide who's who in the picture.

- W's hair is short.
- X has got blonde hair.
- Y's hair is the same length as W's.
- Z never plays tennis.
- W is taller than X.
- W's hair is the same colour as Z's.
- Y's hair is not as long as X's.
- Z is not as tall as X.
- Z's hair is black.
- W wears glasses.
- Z has got long hair.
- X plays tennis with Y.
- Y's hair is the same colour as X's.

6 Time to talk

What's your favourite:

food?
drink?
sport?
colour?
month?
day of the week?
time of the day?
season?
group / singer?

a Write down your answers.

b Discuss your answers in groups.

c Find out which is the most popular food, drink, etc.

7 Now you're here

Your town

Ask a British person the following questions about the town / area where you are staying.

- Is there | a swimming pool?
  a tourist information centre?
  a sports centre?
  a library?
  an amusement arcade?
  a bowling alley?
  a good football team?
  a local newspaper?
  a riding school?

- Are there any | cinemas?
  discos?
  tennis courts?

- What time do shops / banks open?
- What time do they close?
- What day is early closing?
- Do banks open on Saturday?
- Where's the nearest post office?

UNIT TWO
LESSON ONE

First lesson

I'VE GOT A FRIEND. HER NAME'S TESSA. SHE SEEMS NORMAL, BUT IN FACT SHE'S MAD. SHE'S MAD ABOUT ONE THING — WINDSURFING.

IN THE SUMMER SHE GETS UP EARLY AND GOES TO THE BEACH AND WINDSURFS ALL DAY — IF SHE'S LUCKY. IF THERE'S NO WIND, SHE JUST SITS ON THE BEACH AND WAITS. IN THE WINTER SHE DOES THE SAME (BUT IN A WETSUIT). AND *NOW* SHE'S TRYING TO TEACH *ME!*

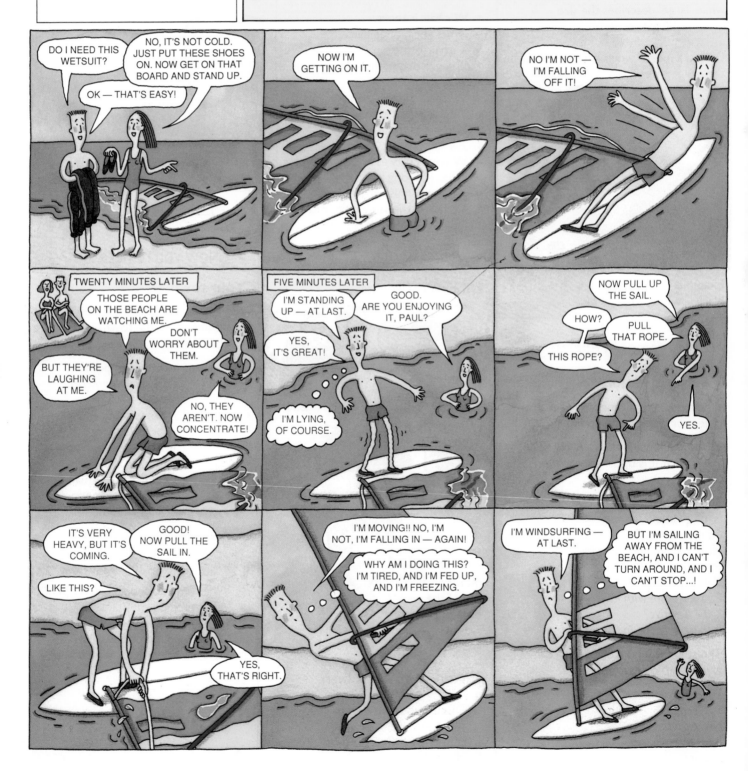

1 What's happening?

a Look at the pictures on page 12 for two minutes.

b Test your memory. Work in pairs. Ask each other questions about what's happening in each of the pictures. Student A asks questions on pictures 1 – 4 and B answers them (without looking at the pictures). Student B asks questions on pictures 5 – 8 and A answers them in the same way.

Example: (Picture 1)
A *What's Tessa doing?*
B *She's talking to Paul.*
A *Is she wearing a wetsuit?*
B *No, she isn't.*
A *What's Paul doing?*
B *He's holding a wetsuit.*

2 Memory game

a All the students in the class look at each other for one minute.

b Students prepare questions like the ones below.

How many students in the class are wearing glasses?
Where's Maki sitting?
What's Manuel wearing?
Who's sitting next to Pia?

c One student at a time stands at the front of the class blindfolded (or with his / her back to the class) and tries to answer the questions other students ask.

3 At work / after work

a Look at these examples:

What does he do? *What's he doing now?*
He teaches. *He's windsurfing.*

b Work in pairs. Ask and answer the same two questions about the other pictures.

1

2

3

4

5

6

c Now ask each other:

- What does your father do?
  What do you think he's doing now?
- What does your mother do?
  What do you think she's doing now?
- What does your sister / brother do?
  What do you think he's / she's doing now?

4 Do what you're told

Listen to the instructions on the cassette and do exactly what the voice tells you to do.

Grammar summary: page 83

1 Using English money

How much is this?

a Work in pairs. Point and ask each other, 'How much is this?'

Example:
It's 43p.

1

2

3

4

b Now do the same with your own English money.

The money game

Look at these things. What is the minimum number of coins you need to pay for these things exactly?

Example: £1.55
Three coins – £1, 50p, 5p

1 £2.09   2 37p   6 17p

4 £3.75   5 73p   3 23p

2 How much are they?

A *How much is a Mars Bar, please?*
B *28p.*
A *And can I have a packet of crisps, please?*
B *That's 51p altogether.*
A *Thanks.*

a Practise this dialogue in pairs.

b Student A 'buys' one or two of the things from Exercise 1 as in the example. Use real money if you want. B must give A the right change.

3 What's missing?

Listen to this dialogue in a shop. Write down the prices of the things the girl buys and then the total cost.

Apples	
Orange	
Seven-up	
Kit Kat	
Biscuits	
Total	

4 Act it out

Work in pairs. Student A is a customer and wants to buy four things for a picnic. Student B is a shopkeeper and tells student A what the things cost. Change roles.

5 Prices

A *How much is a <u>cinema ticket</u> in (<u>France</u>)?*
B *About (<u>30 francs</u>).*
A *How much is that in English money?*
B *About (<u>£3</u>).*

Work in pairs. Talk about your country, and use the words in the box instead of the underlined words.

> a hamburger   a local newspaper
> a litre of milk   an LP   a 50cc moped
> a cup of coffee in a cafe
> a litre of petrol
> a pair of Levi jeans
> a local phone call from a telephone box

6 Asking about and telling the time

What's the time?

Work in pairs. Take it in turns to ask and say what time it is. Use the same questions as in the pictures above.

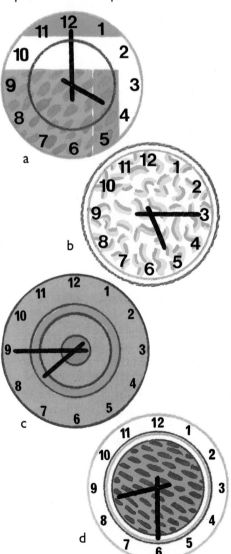

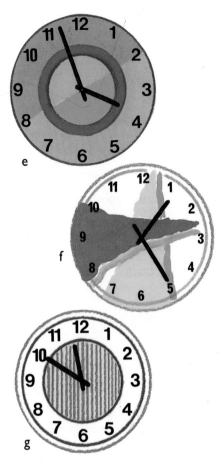

7 What time is it?

Listen to these short conversations and announcements. Write down the time which is mentioned in each of them.

1 ....
2 ....
3 ....
4 ....
5 ....
6 ....

> **Summary of English in situations**
>
> * using English money
> * asking about the price of things
> * asking about and telling the time

1 Sound right

a Which words do not rhyme with the other two?

Example:
(now) show know

1 four hour your
2 goes does shows
3 food rude good
4 their there here
5 put foot but
6 watch catch match
7 quite tight quiet
8 great eight eat

b 🎧 Listen to how the sets of words are pronounced.

c Work in pairs. Take it in turns to pronounce the words. Help and correct each other.

2 Time to talk

What's your excuse?

a Work in groups. Decide on the best excuse or the best solution to the following problems. Use your imagination!

1 You're on a train, and the ticket collector asks you for your ticket. You haven't got one.
2 Your teacher, who is very strict, asks you for your homework. You haven't done it.
3 You're in a cafe. You suddenly realize you haven't got enough money to pay the bill.
4 A boy/girl you don't like phones you up and asks you to go to a party with him/her on Saturday night.

5 You're staying with an English family. You go out in the evening, telling them you'll be home at ten o'clock. You don't come home until one o'clock. They're waiting up for you.

b Each group takes it in turn to give their excuse in each situation. The teacher gives a point to the group with the best excuse in each situation.

3 Read and think

Fast reading test

You've only got five minutes to finish this test so you must work *fast*.
Read all the instructions first.

1 Write your name in the top right-hand corner of a clean piece of paper.
2 Draw a circle around your name.
3 If you are a boy, write the number fifty in the top left-hand corner. If you are a girl, write the same number in the bottom right-hand corner.
4 Draw a square in the middle of the page. Write today's date in the square and underline it.
5 Count out loud backwards from 20 to 0.
6 Do this sum:
four × twelve + two ÷ five − two. Write the answer in the bottom left-hand corner of your paper.
7 Draw a straight line from your name to the answer to number 6.
8 If you were born in a month with the letter 'r' in it, draw a picture of a house in the *empty* corner of the page. If not, draw a picture of a tree.
9 Shout 'I'm the winner!'
10 Don't follow any of the instructions from 2 to 9!

Who was the winner?

4 Work on words

a Finish the sentences under each picture using the adjectives in the box.

bored	thirsty
frightened	hungry
ill	angry
tired	freezing

1 She's ....   2 He's ....

3 She's ....   4 He's ....

5 He's ....   6 She's ....

7 He's ....   8 She's ....

b Work in pairs. Ask each other 'Are you tired/angry?', etc. If the answer is 'Yes, I am', ask 'Why are you (tired)?'

5 Listen to this

a Look carefully at what's happening in the picture.

b 📺 Listen to the description of the picture. There are six mistakes in it. Make notes of the mistakes as you're listening.

Example:
It's 3.15 not 3.30.

1	4 ....
2	5 ....
3	6 ....

6 Now you're here

a What's the name of the nearest shop / building? Ask a British person if necessary.

Example:

	Name
newsagent's	W.H. Smith

1 supermarket	. . .
2 travel agent's	. . .
3 bank	. . .
4 chemist's	. . .
5 cinema	. . .
6 fish and chip shop	. . .
7 sports shop	. . .
8 Chinese or Indian take-away	. . .
9 off-licence	. . .
10 betting shop	. . .

b Write down one or two things you can buy or get from each of the places above.

c Are these shops in your town? What sort of shops are they? What do they sell?

Boots	Currys
Thomas Cook	Snob
W.H. Smith	Marks & Spencer
Habitat	Argos
Dolcis	Halfords
Woolworth's	BHS
Dixons	Next
C & A	J Sainsbury
Nat West	Benetton
Etam	Laura Ashley
Tesco	Burtons
Manfield	Oddbins

UNIT THREE

LESSON ONE

British teenagers – facts and figures

The average British teenager watches a lot of television (19½ hours a week).

A lot of parents think teenagers are lazy. But in fact 57% get up *before* 7.30 a.m. The average British teenager sleeps for 'only' 8 hours 45 minutes a night.

There isn't a queue outside the bathroom of the average British family. Not many teenagers (only 18%) have a bath or shower in the morning. In fact they only have a bath or shower four times a week.

A lot of British teenagers have a steady girlfriend or boyfriend (37%). But 20% never go out with a person of the opposite sex.

Young people in Britain don't get much pocket money (only £2.95 a week on average). But many of them have a part-time job.

There aren't many cinemas left in Britain today because a lot of people prefer to watch films on television or on video. Only 10% of British teenagers go to the cinema once a month or more.

Not many British teenagers smoke. 76% of girls and 78% of boys are non-smokers.

There are a lot of churches and a lot of different religions in Britain, but not many young people (only 11%) go to church regularly.

A lot of girls brush their teeth twice a day or more (78% in fact). Not many boys brush their teeth that often (only 57%). The result? Boys have a lot more fillings (one-third more) than girls.

1 Questions and answers

a Complete the questions with *much* or *many*.

b Work in pairs. Student A asks the questions and student B answers them using: *Not many.* *Change roles.*
Not much.
A lot.

Example:
A *How much television do British teenagers watch?*
B *A lot.*

How	. . . .	television do British teenagers watch?
	. . . .	teenagers get up after 7 o'clock?
	. . . .	sleep do British teenagers get?
	. . . .	teenagers have a bath or shower in the morning?
	. . . .	teenagers have a steady boyfriend / girlfriend?
	. . . .	pocket money do teenagers get?
	. . . .	of them have got part-time jobs?
	. . . .	cinemas are there in Britain?
	. . . .	boys are non-smokers?
	. . . .	different religions are there in Britain?
	. . . .	British teenagers go to church regularly?

2 Same or different?

a In what ways are you different from the average British teenager? In what ways are you the same as the average British teenager?

Example:
I'm different because I smoke, I go to church every Sunday and I have a shower every morning.

I'm the same because I watch a lot of television, I don't get much pocket money and I don't go to the cinema very often.

b Work in pairs. Compare your sentences with your partner's.

3 A survey

a Divide the class into two groups. The students in each group ask each other questions like these:

How many hours' television do you watch a week?
Do you get up before 7.30?

b Work out the answers to questions like these about facts and figures in the text:

What percentage of the group watch more than 19 hours' television a week?
What percentage get up before 7.30?

c Compare the results of your survey with those of other groups.

4 Find out

a Work in pairs. Student A reads the information about Tim below. Student B reads the information about Helen on page 78.

b Student A asks student B questions about Helen and fills in the missing information about her.

Examples:
How many hours a week does she watch television?
What time does she get up?

C Student B asks student A the same questions about Tim and fills in the missing information about him.

Tim   Helen

Watches TV:
18 hours a week . . . .

Gets up:
7.15 . . . .

Has a bath / shower:
five times a week . . . .

Has a steady girlfriend:
yes . . . .

Goes to the cinema:
twice a month . . . .

Brushes his teeth:
once a day . . . .

Smokes:
no . . . .

Goes to church:
twice a year—at Christmas and Easter . . . .

Sleeps:
8½ hours a night . . . .

5 Picture dictation

a [image] Listen to the description of a picture on the cassette. Draw the picture.

b Now work in pairs. Look at your picture and describe it to your partner. He / She checks that it is the same as his / hers.

Grammar summary: page 83

1 Describing where buildings/places are

Match the pictures with the words and phrases in the box.

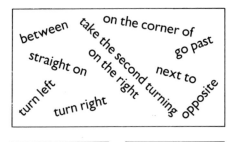

between   on the corner of
take the second turning   go past
straight on   on the right   next to
turn left   opposite
turn right

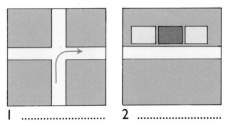

1 ....   2 ....

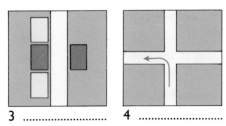

3 ....   4 ....

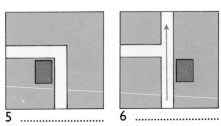

5 ....   6 ....

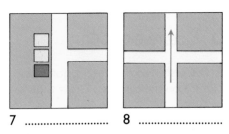

7 ....   8 ....

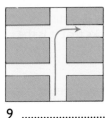

9 ....

2 Where do they want to go?

Listen to the three conversations. They all take place at the station. Follow the directions you hear and draw arrows (→ → →) on the map. Where does each person want to go?

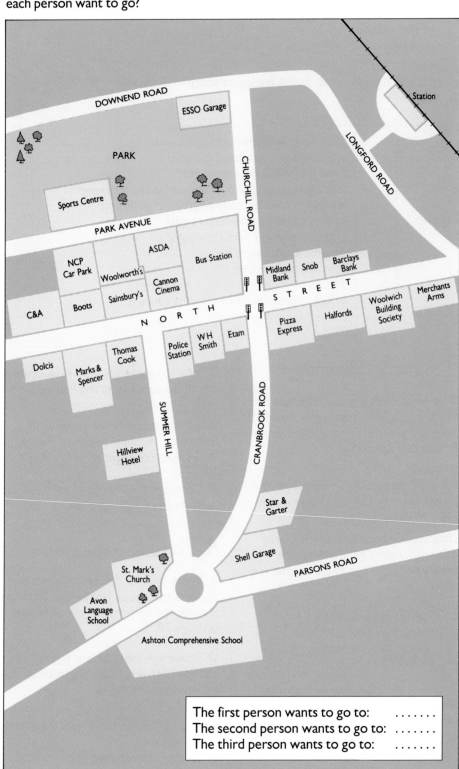

The first person wants to go to: . . . .
The second person wants to go to: . . . .
The third person wants to go to: . . . .

3 Ask and answer

A *Excuse me. Where's the Post Office, please?*
B *It's opposite the station, next to Barclays Bank.*
A *Thanks very much.*
B *You're welcome.*

Work in pairs. Student A asks where a building or place is. Student B describes where it is, using the map. Then student B asks about another building or place and student A answers. Use phrases like these:

A
Thanks.
Thanks a lot.
Thank you.
Thanks very much.
Thank you very much.

B
That's all right.
That's OK.
You're welcome.

Example:
A *Excuse me. Where's the bus station, please?*
B *It's on the corner of Churchill Road and North Street.*
A *Thanks very much.*
B *That's OK.*

4 What's missing?

Work in pairs. Student A looks at the map below, student B looks at the map on page 78. Take it in turns to ask and answer questions. (Student A starts.)

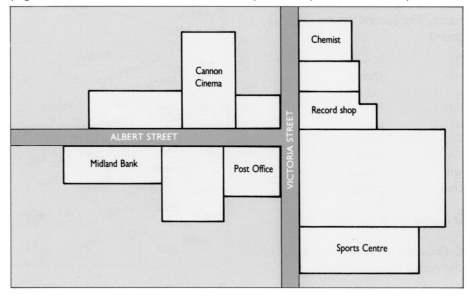

You want to know where these places / buildings are:
1 the park
2 the nearest bus stop
3 St Paul's Church
4 the Red Lion pub
5 a Chinese take-away
6 the Oxford School of English.

Find and mark them on your map with the information you get from student B.

Ask each other questions like this:

A *Excuse me. Where's the nearest bus stop, please?*
B *It's ...*

5 What to say at mealtimes

A *What would you like to drink?*
B *Can I have a glass of squash, please?*
A *Yes, of course.*
C *Help yourself to potatoes.*
B *Right, thanks.*
C *Peas?*
B *Yes, please.*

(pause)

C *Don't wait for me. Please start.*
B *Could you pass the salt, please?*
A *Yes, here you are.*
C *Do you want some gravy?*
B *No thanks.*
C *Would you like some more potatoes?*
B *Yes, please.*

(later)

C *Would you like a second helping?*
B *No thanks. That was very nice.*
C *Are you sure you don't want some more?*
B *No really. It was lovely, but I'm full.*

a Work in groups of three. Read the dialogue. Change roles.

b Act out the situation without looking in the book. Use different foods and drinks if you want to.

Summary of English in situations

- asking about and describing where buildings / places are
- accepting and refusing food at mealtimes

21

1 🖭 Sound right

a Listen to these pairs of words. The first word always has the short [ɪ] sound. The second has the long [iː] sound.

[ɪ]	[iː]
this	these
it	eat
hit	heat
sit	seat
fill	feel
live	leave
will	wheel
chip	cheap

b Listen again and repeat the words.

c Draw six squares and write six of the words from a) in them.

Example:

feel	sit	seat
this	heat	chip
live	fill	eat

d Listen to the teacher, and cross out your words when he/she says them.

Example:

feel	sit	seat
this	heat	chip
live	fill	eat

e When all your words are crossed out, shout BINGO!

f Work in groups. Think of phrases or sentences with as many of the words as possible in them. You get one point for each word you use correctly.

Example:
Eat these cheap chips! (4 points)

2 Work on words

Find the pairs of opposites in the two boxes.

Example:
cold – hot

stupid strong interesting forget in teach same rude fat asleep summer this dry first rich pleased tall cheap dead heavy near on **hot** slow up full pull noisy easy safe buy early

that far wet empty poor remember light **cold** difficult sell awake late down fast annoyed dangerous weak quiet last thin different push clever alive boring learn winter expensive polite short out off

3 Play games in English

Who's X?

a One student (A) goes out of the room. The rest of the class choose one student (X).
Student A comes back in and tries to find out who X is by asking questions.

Examples:
Is X tall?
Is X sitting near the window?
Has X got long hair?
Is X wearing jeans?

The class can only give short Yes/No answers and student A can only ask ten questions.

b Play the same game in pairs.

4 Read and think

a Work out the answers to the following problems.

1 An express train leaves London for Manchester at 9.15 in the morning. It travels at an average of 165 k.p.h. A slow train leaves Manchester for London at 10.30 the same morning. It travels at an average speed of 90 k.p.h. It's 395 km from London to Manchester. Which train is nearer London when they meet, the train from London or the train from Manchester?

2 There are fifty socks, twenty-five black and twenty-five red, in a drawer. It's dark and you want a pair of socks the same colour. What's the smallest number of socks you must take out to make sure you've got a pair of socks the same colour?

3 A man is looking at a photograph. He says, 'This person's father is my father's son. But I haven't got any brothers or sisters.' What relation is the man to the person in the photograph?

b Compare your answers in groups. Explain the correct answers to those students who didn't get them right.

5 Time to talk

a Form groups. In two minutes, think of as many jobs/professions as you can.

b The teacher writes them up on the board.

c One student comes to the front and, without saying anything, chooses one of the jobs.

d The class can ask him/her up to twenty questions but can make only three guesses about what the job is.

Examples:

Is your job	dirty?	Yes, it is.
	dangerous?	No, it isn't.
	important?	
Do you work	outside?	
	alone?	
	with your hands?	
Do you use	a telephone?	Yes, I do.
	a special machine?	No, I don't.
Do you	wear a uniform?	
	help people?	
	earn a lot of money?	

6 Listen to this

Listen to these short conversations and write down where they take place. Choose from the places in the box.

a cinema	a sports centre
a shoe shop	a railway station
a post office	a police station
a bank	an Italian restaurant
a chemist's	a bus station

1 ....
2 ....
3 ....
4 ....
5 ....

7 Now you're here

Mealtimes in Britain

a Observe a British family.

- What time do they have their midday meal/their evening meal?
- Do they eat 'foreign' food, like spaghetti and curries?
- Do they have anything to drink with their meal? (What do they drink?)
- Do they have bread with the meal?
- Do they say a prayer before and after meals?
- Do they use napkins?
- How do they leave their knives and forks when they've finished?
- Do they say 'Good appetite' before they start? (Do they say anything else?)
- Does everyone wait for the 'cook' to start eating?
- What do they say when they leave the table (if anything)?
- What do you find 'strange' about British mealtime customs?
- How are they different from those in your country?

b Compare your observations with other students'.

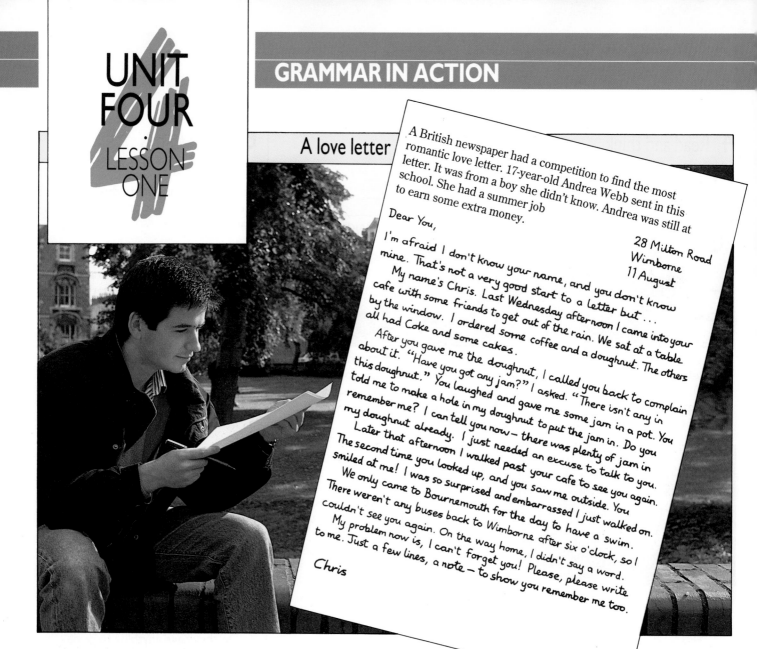

UNIT FOUR
LESSON ONE

A love letter

A British newspaper had a competition to find the most romantic love letter. 17-year-old Andrea Webb sent in this letter. It was from a boy she didn't know. Andrea was still at school. She had a summer job to earn some extra money.

Dear You,

28 Milton Road
Wimborne
11 August

I'm afraid I don't know your name, and you don't know mine. That's not a very good start to a letter but . . .

My name's Chris. Last Wednesday afternoon I came into your cafe with some friends to get out of the rain. We sat at a table by the window. I ordered some coffee and a doughnut. The others all had Coke and some cakes.

After you gave me the doughnut, I called you back to complain about it. "Have you got any jam?" I asked. "There isn't any in this doughnut." You laughed and gave me some jam in a pot. You told me to make a hole in my doughnut to put the jam in. Do you remember me? I can tell you now – there was plenty of jam in my doughnut already. I just needed an excuse to talk to you.

Later that afternoon I walked past your cafe to see you again. The second time you looked up, and you saw me outside. You smiled at me! I was so surprised and embarrassed I just walked on. We only came to Bournemouth for the day to have a swim. There weren't any buses back to Wimborne after six o'clock, so I couldn't see you again. On the way home, I didn't say a word. My problem now is, I can't forget you! Please, please write to me. Just a few lines, a note – to show you remember me too.

Chris

1 What happened when?

In what order did these things happen? Number them 1 – 10.

- [ ] Chris ordered some coffee and a doughnut.
- [ ] Andrea smiled at Chris.
- [ ] Chris went home.
- [1] Chris and his friends came into the cafe.
- [ ] Chris wrote to Andrea.
- [ ] Chris and his friends sat down at a table by the window.
- [ ] Andrea got Chris's letter.
- [ ] Chris walked past the cafe.
- [ ] Andrea gave him some jam.
- [ ] Chris complained about his doughnut.

2 Questions and answers

a Match the questions on the left with the answers on the right.

Example: 1 – e

1 Why did the newspaper have a competition?
2 Why did Andrea have a summer job?
3 Why did Chris come into the cafe?
4 Why did he call Andrea back?
5 Why did Andrea tell Chris to make a hole in his doughnut?
6 Why did Chris walk past the cafe later?
7 Why did Chris and his friends come to Bournemouth?
8 Why does Chris want Andrea to write to him?

a) To show she remembers him.
b) To have a swim.
c) To earn some money.
d) To get out of the rain.
e) To find the most romantic love letter.
f) To put jam in.
g) To complain about his doughnut.
h) To see Andrea again.

b Work in pairs. Student A asks the questions, student B answers them without looking in the book. Change roles.

3 Make true sentences

Example: *Chris wrote a letter to Andrea.*

	(tell)	still at school.
	(sit)	a letter to Andrea.
Chris	(give)	back to Wimborne by bus.
	(write)	by the window.
Andrea	(go)	Chris outside the cafe.
	(send)	Chris some jam.
Chris and his friends	(see)	into the cafe.
	(have)	Chris to make a hole in the doughnut.
	(be)	Chris's letter to a newspaper.
	(come)	a summer job.

4 Role play

Work in pairs. Student A is Chris. He/She reads the instructions below. Student B is Andrea. He/She reads the instructions on page 78.

You are Chris. Andrea didn't reply to your letter. You tried to forget her but you couldn't. A year later you go back to the cafe where you saw her. She's working there again. Tell her who you are. Remind her about the letter you wrote to her. Ask her what she did with it. Tell her you never forgot her. Ask her out.

5 Andrea's letter

a Work in groups of two or three students. Write the letter which you imagine Andrea wrote to Chris. In it, you can tell him:

● how you felt when you got his letter
● what you thought of him when he was in the cafe
● what you thought when he complained about his doughnut
● what you thought when you saw him outside the cafe
● you want to see him again
● where and when you can meet.

b Read out your finished letter to the other groups.

6 What's different?

a Form two teams. Look carefully at this picture of Andy's room for one minute and try to remember everything in it.

b Now turn to the picture on page 79.

7 What have you got?

a Form two or three groups. Each group make a list of the things they've got in their bags/pockets, etc.

Example:
keys   tissues   chewing gum

b Take it in turn to ask other groups what they've got.

Example:
Have you got any keys?
Yes, we have.

You get a point for each object no other group has got.

Grammar summary: page 83

1 🔊 Spelling in English

A *Can I have your name, please?*
B *Kerstin Kjellberg.*
A *Oh goodness! I'm sorry, can you spell that, please?*
B *Yes. K-E-R-S-T-I-N, that's Kerstin. Then K-J-E-L-L-B-E-R-G.*
A *Kerstin Kjellberg. And your address, please?*
B *89, Palmeira Avenue, Hove.*
A *Palmeira, that's P-A-L-M-E-I-R-A, isn't it?*
B *Yes, that's right.*
A *And do you know your postcode?*
B *Yes, it's BN31 7HJ.*
A *Right, I think that's all thanks.*

a Practise the dialogue in pairs. Change roles.

b Practise the dialogue again with another student. Use your own names and addresses.

2 What's the word?

🔊 Write down the letters you hear spelt. What words do they make?

Example:
M-U-S-I-C = music

1	....	6	....
2	....	7	....
3	....	8	....
4	....	9	....
5	....	10	....

3 Spelling game

Form two teams. Ask each other to spell English words.

Example:
Team A *How do you spell 'language'?*
Team B *L-A-N-G-U-A-G-E.*
Team A *Right.* (1 point to Team B)
Team B *How do you spell coffee?*
Team A *C-O-F-E-E.*
Team B *Wrong! C-O-F-F-E-E.* (1 extra point to team B)

4 Pass it on

Form groups of three. Student A thinks of a word and writes it down.

He/She then spells (whispers) it to student B.

Student B writes the word down and spells it (but does not say the word) to student C who also writes it down.

A and C then check that they have the same word.

Student B then thinks of a word.

5 What's missing?

Work in pairs. Student A reads the information below. Student B reads the information on page 79.

Look at the information about these two people. Student B will ask you questions about them.

Name: Salma Kahn
Address: 57 Westerleigh Road
          Leicester LC49 6HQ

Name: Jonathan Davies
Address: 17 Llanfarian Road
          Aberystwyth
          Dyfed AB33 8ZF

Now ask student B questions about these two people and fill in the missing information about them. Ask B to spell any difficult words.

Name: ....
Address: ....
....

Name: ....
Address: ....
....

6 Apologizing

a Practise the dialogue above in pairs. Then use phrases like these:

A	B
Sorry.	*That's all right.*
I'm very sorry.	*Never mind.*
I'm terribly sorry.	*Don't worry.*

b Act out the situations in the pictures. A must apologize to B, and B must accept the apology using the phrases above. Change roles.

1

2

3

4

5

Summary of English in situations

- spelling in English
- apologizing/responding to apologies

27

1 Sound right

a Listen to these pairs of words. What is the difference in pronunciation between the words on the left and the words on the right?

cat	cut
hat	hut
match	much
cap	cup
bat	but
ran	run
sang	sung
fan	fun

b Listen again and repeat the words.

c Now tick (√) the words you hear.

1 but ☐	2 ran ☐	3 cat ☐
bat ☐	run ☐	cut ☐
4 much ☐	5 cup ☐	6 sung ☐
match ☐	cap ☐	sang ☐
7 hat ☐	8 fun ☐	
hut ☐	fan ☐	

d Work in pairs. Student A writes down seven of the words in a) and reads them out to student B. Student B writes them down. Compare your two lists. Change roles.

2 Listen to this

How does the speaker feel in each of these short conversations? Choose from the words in the box.

excited	happy
bored	interested
scared	tired
unhappy	angry
impatient	embarrassed

1 ....
2 ....
3 ....
4 ....
5 ....
6 ....

3 Read and think

This plan shows part of a shopping centre. Read the information about the eight shops and then label them.

- Currys and Dixons both sell electrical goods.
- Etam is at the end of the street.
- Manfield is next to W.H. Smith.
- Boots is opposite Etam.
- W.H. Smith sells newspapers and books.
- Dixons is between Manfield and Etam.
- Boots closes early on Wednesdays.
- Woolworth's is the third shop on the left-hand side.
- Manfield is opposite C & A.
- Boots is a chemist's.
- C & A is between Woolworth's and Currys.

Boots	C & A	Dixons
Manfield	Currys	Etam
W.H. Smith	Woolworth's	

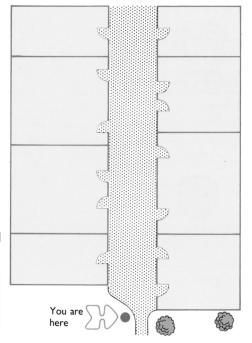

You are here

4 Work on words

What's the missing word?

Examples:
a bed / beds   a life / *lives*
60 seconds / 1 minute   60 minutes / *1 hour*

1 5–12 / a child	13–19 / . . .
2 England / English	Britain / . . .
3 a letter / write	a newspaper / . . .
4 4 weeks / a month	12 months / . . .
5 sons and daughters / children	mother and father / . . .
6 sleep / a bedroom	wash / . . .
7 1st / first	2nd / . . .
8 a person / people	a child / . . .
9 we / our	they / . . .
10 Wednesday / yesterday	Thursday / . . .
11 2 / twice	1 / . . .
12 a school / schools	a church / . . .
13 coffee / drink	a cigarette / . . .
14 ½ / half	⅓ / . . .
15 food / a plate	drink / . . .

5 Time to talk

a Form groups of two or three students. Each group thinks of a simple story which they can mime.

b Each group mimes their story. The rest of the class retell the story using the past tense.

Example:
A boy saw a girl in a disco.   *He went over to her.*   *He asked her to dance.*

She said no.   *He asked why not.*   *She said she was tired.*

The boy went away.   *Another boy asked the girl to dance.*   *She got up and danced.*

6 Play games in English

What's missing?

Form two teams, A and B. The teacher writes up on the board the first and last letters of a word. Each team then tries to think of as many words as they can, beginning and ending with those letters, in one minute.

Example: B . . . . D

Team A	Team B
bad	*bed*
band	*blood*
bored	*bread*
blind	*borrowed*

7 Now you're here

Abbreviations

a Ask a British person what these letters and abbreviations stand for.

VAT	UK
m.p.h.	ITV
k.p.h.	UN
EEC	SOS
BBC	RC
p.m.	ER
a.m.	CIA
AA	DJ
RAC	LP
VIP	PS
MP	e.g.
c/o	c.c.
VHF	p.t.o.
WC	IRA
DIY	UFO

b Collect more abbreviations like these. Ask other students about them the next day.

UNIT FIVE
LESSON ONE

Better or worse?

British schools, twenty or thirty years ago, were very different from the way they are today. Nick Page discovered this when he 'interviewed' his parents for a school project. These are the notes he made.

Were schools better or worse than they are now? You can decide.

NOW  **THEN**

NOW	THEN
Teachers aren't usually very strict. Classes are often noisy and pupils are sometimes rude to teachers.	Teachers were much stricter. Classes were much quieter and there was better discipline. Pupils were more polite to teachers.
Men teachers don't always wear ties. Women teachers sometimes wear trousers or jeans.	Men teachers always wore ties, and women teachers wore skirts or dresses.
We have a kind of uniform but it's very 'free'. Only the colour is important— a green skirt or a grey jumper, for example.	They had much stricter rules about uniform. They all wore the same school tie, school blazer and school cap or hat.
Girls often wear lipstick or eye-shadow, and ear-rings.	The girls never wore make-up or jewellery.
Teachers never hit pupils (but they sometimes put them in detention).	Teachers sometimes hit 'bad' pupils.
Religious studies include religions like Hinduism and Islam, not just Christianity.	Religious studies were always about the Bible and Christianity.
We have boys and girls at the same school, and often at the same desk.	School was more boring. There were hardly ever boys and girls at the same school.
School food is terrible. We all take a packed lunch.	School food was even worse! But they all ate it... they didn't have any choice!
We do 'new' subjects like computer studies and sociology.	The subjects they studied were more traditional.

1 Questions and answers

a Match the questions on the left with the answers on the right.

Example: 1 – c

1 Were British schools very different 30 years ago?
2 Are teachers usually very strict now?
3 Did men teachers always wear ties 30 years ago?
4 Is school uniform stricter now?
5 Do girls wear make-up?
6 Do teachers hit pupils nowadays?
7 Did religious studies only include Christianity?
8 Did boys and girls usually go to the same school?
9 Is school food better nowadays?

a) No, it isn't.
b) No, they didn't.
c) Yes, they were.
d) Yes, they do.
e) No, they aren't.
f) No, they don't.
g) Yes, they did.
h) Yes, it is.
i) Yes, it did.

b Work in pairs. Student A asks the questions. Student B answers them without looking in the book. Change roles.

2 Compare them

Without looking at the text, compare schools thirty years ago with schools today.

Example:
teachers / strict
Thirty years ago, teachers were stricter than today.

1 classes / noisy
2 pupils / polite
3 discipline / good
4 uniform / strict
5 religious studies / interesting
6 school / boring
7 school food / bad

3 Now or then?

🔲 Listen to these short conversations and write down whether you think they took place in a typical school 30 years ago or in a school today. Tick (√) the right answer.

	Now	Then
1		
2		
3		
4		
5		
6		
7		
8		

4 What about your school?

a Make complete sentences about *your* school. Use the words in the box.

Examples:
At my school men teachers always wear ties.
At my school we are never noisy.

always usually often sometimes hardly ever never

b Compare your school with the school where you are learning English now.

c Compare schools in your country with those of students from other countries.

5 School subjects

a Which of these subjects do you study at school? Mark your answer with a tick (√) or a cross (×) in column (A).

	(A) √ or ×	(B) Important	(C) Enjoyable
English			
Maths			
Physics			
History			
Your own language			
Music			
P.E. (physical education)			
Biology			
Religious studies			
Chemistry			
Geography			
Art			
Latin			

b Now choose what you think are the five most important subjects and order them 1 to 5 in column (B).

c Now choose the five most enjoyable subjects and number them 1 to 5 in column (C).

d Work in pairs. You have five minutes to try to make your partner agree with your order.

Example:
I don't agree. I think English is much more important than Latin.
Yes, but I think it's less important than maths.

6 Guessing game

a The teacher names two students in the class (two who look similar, if possible).

b The teacher asks questions:

Examples:

Who do you think is older?
Who do you think is taller?
Who do you think is lighter?

Who do you think has got bigger feet?
Who's better at drawing?
Who's better at singing?

Write down your answers.

c Check to see who has guessed the most right answers.

Grammar summary: page 84

31

I Telephoning

Using a payphone

Match the instructions with the pictures and fill in the blanks below them.

- Put your money in.
- Dial the number you want.
- Pick up the receiver and listen for dialling tone.
- Don't forget to take your unused coins back.
- Have your money ready (10p, 50p, £1).
- Speak when somebody answers.

1 ....

2 ....

3 ....

4 ....

5 ....

6 ....

Using a cardphone

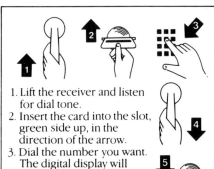

1. Lift the receiver and listen for dial tone.
2. Insert the card into the slot, green side up, in the direction of the arrow.
3. Dial the number you want. The digital display will show the number of unused units on the card. Listen for the ringing tone and speak when connected.
4. When you finish your call, replace the receiver and the card will be ejected automatically.
5. Retrieve the card.

How to make an international call

1 Dial 010.

2 Dial the code for your country.
Examples:
France 33   Italy 39   Spain 34
Germany 49   Japan 81   Brazil 55

3 Now dial the code for the town/city you want (usually without the first figure).
Examples:
Athens 1   Stockholm 8
Barcelona 3

4 Finally, dial the number of the person you want to speak to.

Now write down the full number of your own family (or a friend in your country) if you want to phone them from Britain.

010	34	1	4476807
international code	country code (Spain)	city code (Madrid)	number of family, friend, etc.

2 Cashing traveller's cheques

A *Can I cash these traveller's cheques, please?*
B *Yes, certainly. Have you got any means of identification, please?*
A *Sorry?*
B *Have you got your passport?*
A *Oh, no. But I've got my identity card. Is that all right?*
B *Yes, that's fine. Can you sign the cheques, please, and fill in the date.*
A *Yes, of course.*
B *How would you like the money?*
A *Sorry?*
B *Do you want it in fives or tens?*
A *Fives, please.*

Practise the conversation above in pairs. A is the student, B is the bank clerk. Change roles.

3 Changing money

A *Can I help you?*
B *Yes, I'd like to change these Spanish pesetas into pounds, please.*
A *Certainly.*

(counts)

A *That's 10,000 pesetas altogether in notes. But I'm afraid we can't change the coins.*
B *Oh, I see.*
A *Now, can you write your name and address on this form, please?*
B *My address in England or in Spain?*
A *Your address in England.*

(pause)

Thank you. How would you like the money—in fives or tens?
B *In tens, please . . . Thank you.*

Practise the dialogue above in pairs. Change the underlined words if necessary. Change roles.

4 Days and dates

Listen to the short conversations on the cassette. Write down the dates which you hear.

Example: 7 / 6 / 67

1 ....
2 ....
3 ....
4 ....

5 A survey

a Each student in the class writes down on a piece of paper the twelve months of the year.

b Students then go round the class asking, 'When's your birthday?' Tick (√) the month for each answer and add the date.

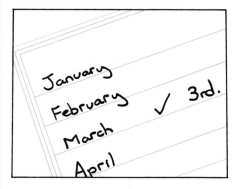

- Which month is the most popular for birthdays?
- Which month is the least popular?
- Are there any students in the class with the same birthday?

Note: You *write* 21 (st) August, 1989 or 21/8/89.
You *say* 'The twenty-first of August, nineteen eighty-nine.'

6 A quiz

a Form two teams. The teacher asks the questions below. Students have their books closed. The first team to answer correctly get a point.

- What's the day before Thursday?
- What's the day after Monday?
- What's the day between Friday and Sunday?
- It's Wednesday today. What day is it tomorrow?
- What day was it yesterday?
- In which day is the third letter D?
- What is the month before October?
- Which month comes between January and March?
- In which month is the third letter P?
- In which month is the last letter L?
- Which is the shortest month of the year?
- Which month has the longest day?
- Which month has the shortest name?
- Which month has the longest name?
- Which month doesn't always have the same number of days?
- Which three months begin with the same letter?

b Ask each other more questions like those in a).

Summary of English in situations
• using a payphone and making an international phone call • cashing traveller's cheques • changing money • talking about days / dates

33

1 Sound right

a Listen to these words from the text on page 30.

British	project	discipline
ago	uniform	teacher
today	detention	discovered
parents	terrible	Christianity
jewellery	twenty	women
polite	student	religious
decide	trousers	boring
usually		

b Listen again and underline the stressed or heavy syllables.

Example: <u>Bri</u>tish

c Now read the words with as much stress or emphasis as possible on the syllables you underlined.

2 Work on words

Find words in the first box which mean the same or almost the same as the words in the second box.

Example:
hi – hello

crazy	freezing	**hello**
OK	terrible	small
fast	cheerio	too
nice	large	angry
hard	a lot of	scared

quick	fine	little
also	**hi**	annoyed
many	mad	goodbye
big	cold	difficult
lovely	afraid	horrible

3 Listen to this

Listen to the short conversations between shoppers and a woman at the information desk in a big department store. Write down the missing information in the table.

	Wants to buy	Floor
1st customer		
2nd customer		
3rd customer		
4th customer		
5th customer		

4 Time to talk

a Tick (✓) your answers to these statements.

	I agree	I don't agree
1 Boys are more interested in sport than girls.	☐	☐
2 Boys are better at maths and science than girls.	☐	☐
3 Girls are better at languages than boys.	☐	☐
4 Boys are noisier than girls.	☐	☐
5 Girls are more hard-working than boys.	☐	☐
6 Teachers pay more attention to boys than girls (i.e. they ask them more questions).	☐	☐
7 Boys cheat more often than girls in tests and exams.	☐	☐
8 Girls are 'teacher's pets' more often than boys.	☐	☐
9 Girls are more mature than boys of the same age.	☐	☐

b Compare and discuss your answers in groups.

5 Read and think

There are three jokes below, but they are mixed up.

Write out the three complete jokes.

1 Two fleas came out of a cinema. One said to the other,
2 'Where to?' asked the clerk.
3 'Be careful! You've got your thumb in my soup.'
4 'Back here, of course!'
5 A woman went into a railway station.
6 'It's all right,' he answered. 'It's not very hot.'
7 'Shall we walk home?'
8 'Can I have a return ticket, please?' she said.
9 A customer in a restaurant said to the waiter,
10 'No, I'm tired', said the other. Let's take a dog.'

6 Play games in English

Quick changes

a Form two teams, A and B.

b The teacher writes a short word up on the board.

c A member of team A makes a new word by changing only one letter. (They must know what the new word means!)

d A member of team B does the same. The game continues until one team can't change the word on the board. When this happens the other team wins and the teacher starts the game again with a different word.

7 Now you're here

Ask a British person these questions.

How often do you go to:
church?
the dentist's?
a pub?
the cinema?
the theatre?
the hairdresser's?
a restaurant?

How often do you:
have a take-away meal?
go out in the evening?
get some form of exercise? (What do you do?)
have a holiday?
go abroad? (Where do you go?)

UNIT SIX · LESSON ONE

You know it's over when . . .

. . . she gets up, just as you're going to sit down next to her.

. . . they play *your* record (the one you enjoy dancing to together) at a party or disco and he just says, 'I'm tired, I'm going to sit down.'

. . . she says, 'No, I can't see you this evening. I'm going to wash my hair.' (For the fourth time that week!).

. . . she says she's going home because she feels tired—at eight o'clock in the evening!

. . . her mother says she's going to phone you back, after her bath, but she never does. And when you phone again, she's never there.

. . . he's going away for a few days, and you tell him 'I'm going to miss you', and he just answers, 'Yes, I know.'

. . . you say, 'Are we going for a walk then—you and me?' and he just says, 'No, you can go. I like being with the others.'

. . . she says she's going to watch a football match tomorrow, but you know she *hates* watching football!

1 Make sentences

Match the first part of the sentence on the left with the second half on the right.

Example: 1 – f

You know it's over when:

1 . . . she gets up
2 . . . her mother say's she's going to phone you back after her bath
3 . . . they play *your* record at a party or disco
4 . . . you say, 'Are we going for a walk then, you and me?'
5 . . . he's going away for a few days and you tell him 'I'm going to miss you'
6 . . . she says she's going home because she feels tired
7 . . . she says, 'No, I can't see you this evening. I'm going to wash my hair.'
8 . . . she says she's going to watch a football match

a) at eight o'clock in the evening.
b) but he just says, 'I'm tired. I'm going to sit down.'
c) and he just says, 'No, you can go. I like being with the others.'
d) but you know she *hates* watching football.
e) but she never does. And when you phone again she's never there.
f) just as you're going to sit down next to her.
g) and he just answers, 'Yes, I know.'

h) —for the fourth time that week.

2 What are they going to do?

Describe what's going to happen in each of these pictures.

Example:
She's going to answer the phone.

1

2

3

4

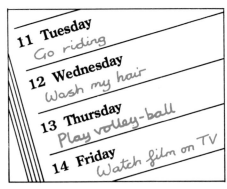

5

3 What are you going to do?

a Write a diary like this with things you're probably going to do in the next four days (but not just the things on the course programme).

11 Tuesday
Go riding
12 Wednesday
Wash my hair
13 Thursday
Play volley-ball
14 Friday
Watch film on TV

b Go round the class asking and answering questions like this:

What are you going to do on Wednesday?
I'm going to play volley ball.

c Make a list of students who are going to do the same thing on the same day as you. The student with the most names is the winner.

4 Does she like him?

This is Suzanne's diary for the next few days.

11 Tuesday
Hairdresser's 2:30
Meet S to buy mum's present.
Doctor's 6:15
12 Wednesday
Driving lesson 2:45
Dance class 7:30
13 Thursday
Mum's birthday

Now listen to this telephone conversation and decide if Suzanne wants to go out with Dave or not. Are all her excuses 'true' or not? If not, which excuse is not genuine?

5 Tell a lie

a Write three sentences beginning:

I love . . .
I enjoy . . .
I hate . . .

Two sentences must be true, one a lie.

Examples:
I love getting up in the morning.
I enjoy ironing.
I hate having a cold shower.

b Read out your sentences to the class. They decide which one is a lie.

Grammar summary: page 85

1 Clothes

jacket
T-shirt
boots
tights
jumper
belt
socks
knickers
jeans
dress
bra
blouse
suit
tie
necklace
pyjamas
nightdress
bracelet
skirt
gloves
hairslide
swimsuit
trainers
underpants
coat
shirt
trousers
sweater
scarf
shorts
sunglasses
ring (s)
ear ring (s)

a Put a symbol after each word like this:

☑ if you're wearing it now.
⊟ if you're not wearing it now but you've got it in Britain.
◻ if you've got it at home in your country but not with you in Britain.
☒ if you haven't got it or never wear it.

b Now mark the words with these symbols:
♀ if they are usually worn by girls or women.
♂ if they are usually worn by boys or men.
☿ if they are worn by both sexes.

Compare your lists with other students'.

2 ☎ Shopping for clothes

Assistant *Can I help you?*
Customer *No, I'm just looking thanks.*

(two minutes later)

Customer *Excuse me. Have you got these jeans in my size?*
Assistant *What size are you?*
Customer *I'm 85 waist, I think.*
Assistant *85. That's 34 inches.*

(pause)

Assistant *These are all 34 waist.*
Customer *Can I try these on, please?*
Assistant *Yes, of course. The changing rooms are over there.*

(later)

Assistant *Yes, they suit you.*
Customer *But I'm afraid they don't fit me. They're too big. Have you got a size smaller?*
Assistant *Yes, these are size 32.*

(later)

Customer *Yes, these are fine. I'll have them, thanks. How much are they?*
Assistant *They're £24.95 . . . Anything else?*
Customer *No, that's all thanks.*

Act out this dialogue in pairs. Change roles.

Sizes

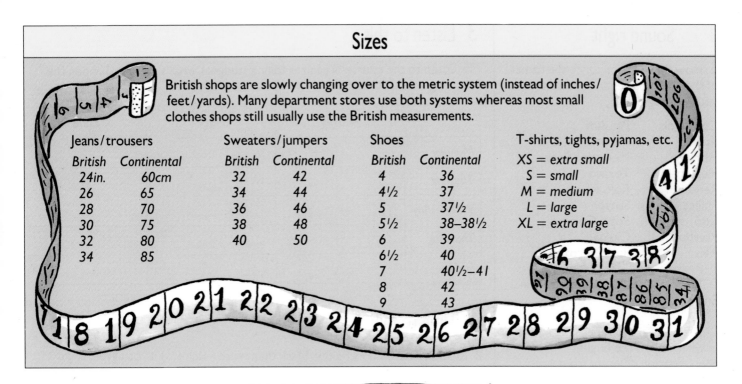

British shops are slowly changing over to the metric system (instead of inches/feet/yards). Many department stores use both systems whereas most small clothes shops still usually use the British measurements.

Jeans/trousers		Sweaters/jumpers		Shoes		T-shirts, tights, pyjamas, etc.
British	Continental	British	Continental	British	Continental	XS = extra small
24in.	60cm	32	42	4	36	S = small
26	65	34	44	4½	37	M = medium
28	70	36	46	5	37½	L = large
30	75	38	48	5½	38–38½	XL = extra large
32	80	40	50	6	39	
34	85			6½	40	
				7	40½–41	
				8	42	
				9	43	

3 What's wrong?

Work in pairs. Imagine you want to buy the things in the pictures.

Act out the dialogues. Use phrases like:

It's		big
	too	small.
They're		long.
		short.
		tight.
		expensive.

They're too big.

4 What do they buy?

Listen to the cassette and fill in the missing information in the table below.

	Item of clothing	Colour	Size	Price
First customer				
Second customer				
Third customer				

5 Role play

Work in pairs. Student A reads the instructions below. Student B reads the instructions on page 80.

You want to buy a jumper (size 36).

You like red and dark blue best. You only really want to spend £15.

Talk to the shop assistant. Ask him/her about colours, size, prices, etc.

Start like this:
I'm looking for a jumper . . .

Summary of English in situations

- buying clothes
- talking about sizes and colours

1 ▣ Sound right

a How do you pronounce the names of these companies and products in your language?

Coca-Cola	Pan Am
Kodak	Hilton Hotels
Honda	Mercedes Benz
McDonald's	Texaco
Renault	Rolls Royce
Philips	Sanyo
Esso	Pepsi-Cola
Marlboro	Citroën
Avis	Rank Xerox

b Now listen to how they sound in English.

c Listen again and repeat the names. In what ways is the English pronunciation different from your language?

d Work in groups. Think of other international companies or products. Try to pronounce them in an English way. Check your pronunciation with your teacher.

2 Read and think

a Read through the following conversation.

'Where's Pia?' asked the teacher.
'She's not here,' said Jaime.
'I can see that,' said the teacher.
'Where is she?'
'I don't know,' said Daniel.
'I haven't seen her,' said Christina.
'She's ill in bed,' said Sonia.
'That's right,' said Martine. 'She's got a bad cold.'
'No, she hasn't,' said Paul. 'She's gone shopping.'
'That's not true!' said Louise.

b All the students except one told the truth. Who was lying and where was Pia?

3 Listen to this

▣ Listen to the course organizer telling students what's going to happen the following week. Fill in the table below.

	Activity	Place	Time
Monday			
Tuesday			
Wednesday			
Thursday			
Friday			

4 Time to talk

a Read the statements below. Mark them with a tick (√) if you agree, and a cross (✕) if you don't agree.

1 'British people wear nice clothes.' ☐
2 'Clothes are cheaper in Britain than in my country.' ☐
3 'I'm not really interested in clothes.' ☐
4 'I love window-shopping.' ☐
5 'I get ideas for my clothes from magazines.' ☐
6 'I spend most of my money on clothes.' ☐
7 'I don't want to look different—I want to look the same as other people my age.' ☐
8 'I never wear the same clothes two days running.' ☐
9 'I dress for myself, not for the opposite sex.' ☐
10 'I decide what clothes to buy and wear, not my parents.' ☐
11 'I think it's OK for boys to wear ear rings.' ☐

b Work in pairs. Guess what your partner's answers were before you discuss them.

5 Play games in English

Word tennis

Form two teams, A and B. The teacher chooses a word. Team A think of a word associated with that word, team B a word associated with A's word and so on.

Example:
Teacher *hungry*
Team A *food*
Team B *eat*
Team A *dinner*
Team B *evening*
Team A *night*
Team B *sleep*
Team A *bed*
etc.

If one team can't think of a word in five seconds, the other team wins a point.

6 Work on words

1 spoon
2 corkscrew
3 knife
4 fork
5 bottle opener
6 needle
7 hairdrier
8 hammer
9 key
10 plug
11 screwdriver
12 comb
13 torch
14 razor
15 toothbrush
16 scissors
17 tin opener

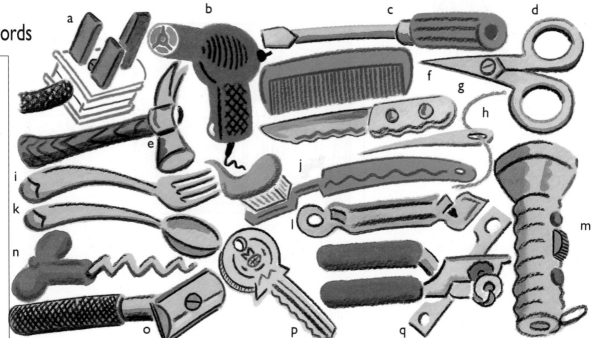

a Match the words in the box with the correct pictures.

Example: 1–k

b Work in groups. Ask each other what the things above are used for.

Example:
What do you use a knife for?
You use a knife to cut.

c Test your memory. Work in pairs. Student B closes his/her book. Student A asks questions.

Examples:
What do you call a thing for opening bottles?
What do you call a thing for cleaning your teeth?

Change roles after three minutes.

7 Now you're here

Ask a British person what these signs and notices mean and where you see them.

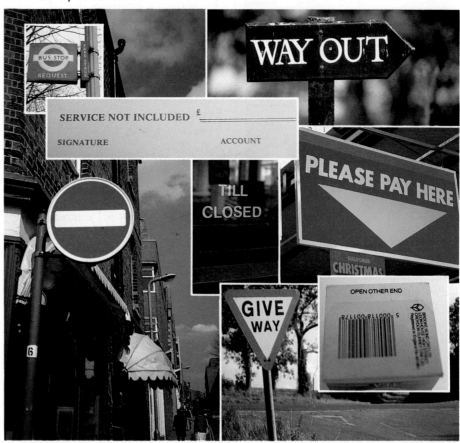

UNIT SEVEN
LESSON ONE

You can be sure . . .

If you come home and the phone is ringing, don't hurry. You can be sure it'll stop ringing the moment before you answer it.

Now which of these are true for you?

If you kill the last mosquito in your bedroom before you go to sleep, its friend will always bite you, just after you go to sleep.

If you take something—like a radio or cassette player—back to the shop because it's broken, it'll work perfectly.
Or you'll find that the guarantee is *just* out of date.

If you find a pair of jeans or shoes you really like, the shop won't have them in *your* size.
If they *have* got them in your size, they'll always be the most expensive in the shop, or the worst colour.

If you're in a building with double doors, you'll always *push* the door you should *pull* (or *pull* the door you should *push*).

If you choose one queue in a supermarket because it's the shortest, the other queues will always move faster.
If you change queues, the queue you were in before will *now* move the fastest.

1 What'll happen if . . .?

What will happen in these situations (if you're always unlucky)?

a Write your answers.

Examples:
If you're at a barbecue, the charcoal won't light.
or
If you're at a barbecue, the smoke will always get in your eyes.

1 If you see a boy / girl you really like, . . .
2 If you put some money in an automatic machine, . . .
3 If you go to the cinema, . . .
4 If you try to repair something, . . .
5 If you choose a trolley in a supermarket, . . .
6 If you want to write a letter and you finally find a pen, . . .
7 If you eat spaghetti, . . .
8 If you buy somebody a present, . . .

b Work in groups. Compare your sentences.

2 What are they saying?

What do you think these people are saying? Begin each sentence: 'If . . .'

1

2

3

4

5

6

3 Advice to a foreign visitor

a Form groups. Think of advice for another foreign student coming to Britain for the first time.

Examples:
If you come to Britain,

you'll need an umbrella.
you won't need sunglasses.

b Compare your advice with other groups'.

c In different groups, complete these sentences with advice to a British person visiting your country.

If you come to my country, you'll . . .
you won't . . .

d Compare your advice with that of other groups.

4 Superstitions

a Work in groups. Write complete sentences for common superstitions in your country.

Examples:
You'll have bad luck if you . . .

break a mirror.
walk under a ladder.

b Write similar sentences for superstitions which bring you good luck.

Example:
If you catch a falling leaf, you'll have good luck.

c Which group has the most sentences? If there are students of different nationalities in the class, find out if superstitions are the same in other countries.

5 Your best and your worst

Form groups. Compare your answers to these questions. Say why you answer the way you do.

1 What's the best/worst time of the day?
2 What's the best/worst day of the week?
3 What's the best/worst month of the year?
4 What's the best/worst season?
5 What's the best age to be?

6 Who's the champion?

Form groups of 4–5 students. Find out:

Round 1   Who's the oldest?
Round 2   Who's the youngest?
Round 3   Who's got the biggest family (the most brothers and sisters)?
Round 4   Who's the best at drawing a perfect circle?
Round 5   Who's the best at drawing a straight line, (about 50 cm) on the board?
Round 6   Who's the fastest at writing the English numbers 1–10 with letters (one, two, etc.)?
Round 7   Who's got the longest first name?
Round 8   Who's got the shortest surname?
Round 9   Who's got the longest hair?
Round 10   Who's got the dirtiest shoes?
Round 11   Who's got the smallest feet?
Round 12   Who's the best at English?

The winner of each round gets 3 points. The student who's second gets 2 points and the one who's third gets 1 point.

Grammar summary: page 85

43

1 📺 Telephoning— telephone numbers

A Mrs Stewart, your phone number's five-two-two-eight-four-three, isn't it?

B Yes, that's right. But we say five-double two-eight-four-three. And the code for Bristol's oh-two-seven-two.

A Is 'oh' the same as zero?

B Yes, that's right.

2 What are their numbers?

📺 Listen to these short conversations and write down the telephone numbers you hear mentioned.

1 ....
2 ....
3 ....
4 ....
5 ....

3 Quick questions

Go round the class and ask each other, 'What's your telephone number?' Write down the students' names and numbers. The winner is the student with the most correct telephone numbers after three minutes. (You can give your telephone number in Britain or in your country.)

4 What's missing?

Work in pairs. Student A reads the instructions below. Student B reads the instructions on page 80.

Find out the missing telephone numbers from student B.

Ask questions like this:
What's A.B. Daley's phone number?

```
Dale T.C, 89 Church Rd,Sandford On Thames ....... Oxford 774387
Dale T.C, 9 Maple Rd............................... Bicester 253898
Dale T.C, 5 White Wy ............................ Kidlington 71528
Dale T.J, 22 Morton Clo ......................... Kidlington 2946
Dale W.F, 48 High St ............................. Kidlington 4883
Dale Windows, Unit 2 Fitzharris Trading Est ...... Abingdon 30237
Dale W.M, The Flat 5 St. Leonards Ct ......... Wallingford 36498
Dale-Emberton R.A, 13 Kings Orchard,
              Brightwell-cum-Sotwell ..Wallingford 33640
Dale-Green C.J, 58 Butler Clo ....................Oxford 53390
Dales,International Road Haulage,Twyford ....... Banbury 811441
Dales Cash Stores Ltd, High St .................. Didcot 812221
Dales G.A, 13 Sunnyside,Hollow Wy ............. Oxford 779045
Dales R, 20 Flatford Pl.......................... Kidlington 79114
Dales R, 47 Selwyn Cres,Radley ................. Abingdon 27908
D'Alessandro C.Talbot, 4 Squitchey La ............Oxford 58467
Daley A.B, Downham Cott,Asthall ...........................
Daley B, 25 Spruce Rd........................... Kidlington 6311
Daley C.J, 29 Witan Wy.......................... Wantage 4372
Daley J.J, 1 Belvedere Rd,Cowley ............... Oxford 725735
Daley M.S, 48 Witan Wy ......................... Wantage 4457
Daley P.A, Stanton Ho..................... Stanton St. John 807
Daley R.D, 5 Childrey Wy,E Challow .............. Wantage 3810
Daley R.M,
       Manor Cott,Horton-cum-Studley ..Stanton St. John 442
Daley S.J, 2 Flatford Pl ......................... Kidlington 6961
Daley T, 23 Abbotts Clo ......................... Didcot 812555
Daley W, Snowdrop Ldge,Mill La ............. Upper Heyford 2304
Dalgarno J.A, 14 Otwell Clo ..............................
DALGETY AGRICULTURE Ltd,Agric Mrcnt,
                     Edward St ..Banbury 4477
Dalgleish C.J, 11 Thames Mead ................Wallingford 37061
Dalgleish M,
       Foxcombe Rse,Foxcombe Dv,Boars Hill ..Oxford 730330
Dalgleish T, 380 Marston Rd ....................Oxford 722776
Dalitz R.H, 28 Jack Straws La,Headington ........Oxford 62531
D'All S.J, 22 Richens Dv ........................ Carterton 843457
Dallaire R, Kennel Cott......................... Nettlebed 641925
Dallal E.S, 12 Masefield Cres,Tithe Fm .......... Abingdon 25697
Dallas A, 92 Fernhill Rd,Begbroke ................ Kidlington 4272
Dallas Brett,Solrs—
       25 Beaumont St........................... Oxford 513557
Dallas Brett,Solrs, 25 Beaumont St................. Oxford 513557
Dallas C, 75 Iffley Rd ..................................
Dallas Keith Chemical & Eng Ltd,
       Bromag Indust Est,Burford Rd,Minster Lovell ..Witney 73061
Dallas Keith Ltd,
       Bromag Indust Est,Burford Rd,Minster Lovell ..Witney 73061
Dallas Management Services Ltd, 8 South Pde...... Oxford 514142
```

```
Daly Rev Eltin, 18 Leopold St ..................... Oxford 240325
Daly E.T, 55 Lark Down ........................... Wantage 68408
Daly H.A, 1 Park Cotts,Lower Greenfields,
                  Christmas Com ..Watlington 2046
Daly J, 19 Blenheim Gdns,Grove .................. Wantage 69843
Daly J, 12 Hill Rd ............................... Watlington 2556
Daly J, 21 Hillview ......................................
Daly J.F,
  Corpus Christi Fm Ho,Sandford Rd,Littlemore ..Oxford 715156
Daly J.F, Corpus Christi Farm Ho,Sandford Rd,
                         Littlemore ..Oxford 773779
Daly K.J, 19 Abingdon Rd,Tubney ....... Frilford Heath 390882
Daly Michael, 7 Goodson Wlk .................... Oxford 724105
Daly M, 39 Marston St........................... Oxford 728203
Daly M, 68 Rosamund Rd,Wolvercote ............. Oxford 515990
Daly M.J, 104 Lime Wlk..........................Oxford 68955
Daly M.P, 35 The Grates,Cowley ................. Oxford 771455
Daly N, 6 Blencowe Clo.......................... Bicester 243263
Daly Dr N.A, 93 Rose Hill ....................... Oxford 775445
Daly PC, Maytree Cott,Astall ...................... Burford 3571
Daly R, 115 Holloway,Cowley ................... Oxford 776814
Daly T, 80 Cherwell Rd,Berinsfield ............... Oxford 340973
Daly T, 40 The Firs .................................Brill 238397
Daly T.G.C, 49 Hedgemead Av ................. Abingdon 27448
Daly V.C, 1,Clearfield Cott,Wotton .................Brill 237050
Dalzell W, 7 Barbary Dv,Grove ............................
Dalziel A, 27 Francis Little Dv .................. Abingdon 32291
Dalziel Keith, 25 Hampden Dv ................. Kidlington 2623
Dalziel M.S, 368 Woodstock Rd ..................Oxford 58969
Dalziel S, 29 Tweed Cres ...................... Bicester 244901
Dalziel T.W, 6 Hampden Rd ..................... Wantage 67504
Daman P.J, Church Cott,Shilton ...........................
Damerell C, 4 Godfrey Clo ..................... Abingdon 23418
D'amico M, 141 Corn St ......................... Witney 72869
Damjanovic L, 301 Cowley Rd................... Oxford 725429
Damm F.P, 11 Grange Pk .................... Steeple Aston 47269
Dammarell L.M, 49a Queens Rd ................ Carterton 845066
Damms B.J, 7 Park End ......................... Croughton 810112
Damnjanovic M, 22 Fieldside,Upton ............. Blewbury 850991
Damnjanovic P, 40 Mowbray Rd .................. Didcot 816273
Damp Guard & Timbertech, 45 West St,Osney ...... Oxford 241648
Dampa Ltd,Acoustic Ceiling Mfrs,
          Wimblestraw Rd,Berinsfield ..Oxford 340471
Dampa Marine Ltd, Wimblestraw Rd,Berinsfield .. Oxford 340842
DAMPCURE-WOODCURE /30,Damp,Timb Treatment—
  Branches,
     30 Wendover Rd .........................Aylesbury 85411
Dampness Analysis Ltd,Bldg Dampness Conslt,
            Friars Cott,Market Sq ..Princes Risboro 3535
```

5 Speaking on the phone

A Hello. 305658.

B Hello. Can I speak to Sarah, please?

A Yes, speaking. Who's that?

B It's Peter.

A Oh, hi Peter. How are you?

Practise this dialogue in pairs using your own names and telephone numbers. Change roles.

6 Telephone messages

A 857330.

B Hello. Can I speak to Paco, please?

A No, I'm afraid he's not in. Can I take a message?

B Yes. Can you ask him to ring me, please?

A OK. Who's speaking, please?

B This is Anna.

A All right Anna. I'll tell him. Has he got your number?

B No, I don't think so. It's 354497.

A Just a moment . . . 354497?

B That's right. Thanks very much.

7 Take the messages

Listen to the three telephone conversations on the cassette. Fill in the gaps in the messages.

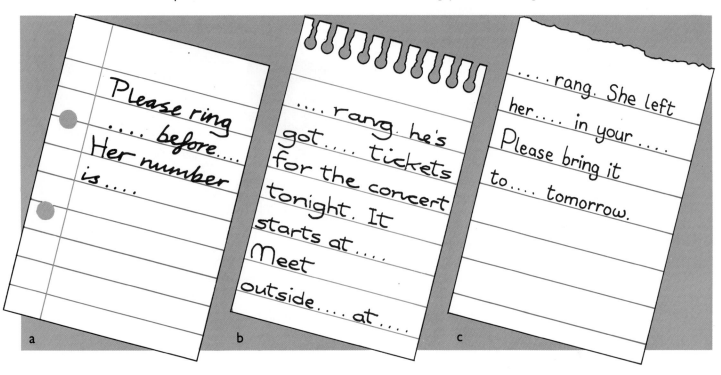

a

Please ring
.... before....
Her number
is ....

b

.... rang. he's
got .... tickets
for the concert
tonight. It
starts at ....
Meet
outside.... at ....

c

.... rang. She left
her.... in your ....
Please bring it
to.... tomorrow.

8 Leave a message

a Form groups of five or six students and sit in a line. The first student in a line (A) writes a telephone message on a piece of paper. The message should include:

- A's name
- the time A wants to meet X
- the place A wants to meet X
- what X should bring (e.g a tennis racket, a cassette, a friend, etc.).

b Student A 'rings' the next student in the line (B), and whispers the message to him/her. Student B then whispers the message to the next student (C), etc.

c The student at the end of the line (X) writes down the message. Students A and X then compare their messages. Are they the same?

Example:

Hans rang. He wants to
meet you outside the
Odeon cinema at 8.15.
He wants you to bring
the books he lent you.

Summary of English in situations

- using the telephone
- telephone numbers
- taking messages on the telephone

1 🎧 Sound right

a Listen to these pairs of words.

1 ☐ sin   2 ☐ sink
  ☐ thin   ☐ think

3 ☐ sick   4 ☐ sank
  ☐ thick   ☐ thank

5 ☐ sort   6 ☐ some
  ☐ thought   ☐ thumb

b Listen again and repeat the pairs of words.

c Now listen and tick the words you hear.

d Listen to these pairs of words.

1 thin   2 three   3 thank
  tin   tree   tank

4 through   5 taught   6 team
  true   thought   theme

e Listen again and repeat the words.

f Draw six squares and write six of the words from a) and d) in them.

true	some	team
tree	sank	thumb

g Now listen to the teacher, and cross out your words when he/she says them. When all your words are crossed out, shout BINGO!

~~true~~	some	team
~~tree~~	sank	thumb

h Work in groups. Practise saying these 'tongue-twisters':

Three thick trees.
Sing something simple.
It's his thirty-third birthday on Thursday.

Who can say them the fastest without making a mistake?

2 Work on words

a Put a tick (√) after the right answers and a cross (✕) after the wrong answers.

1 All boys have
sisters ☐
aunts ☐
mothers ☐
cousins ☐
uncles ☐
fathers. ☐

2 All rooms have
chairs ☐
tables ☐
walls ☐
windows ☐
furniture ☐
shelves. ☐

3 All books have
pictures ☐
pages ☐
words ☐
authors ☐
covers ☐
indexes. ☐

4 All girls have
eye-shadow ☐
lipstick ☐
ear rings ☐
make-up ☐
mouths ☐
noses. ☐

5 All teenagers
swim ☐
smoke ☐
sleep ☐
dance ☐
drink ☐
complain. ☐

6 All meals have
ketchup ☐
vegetables ☐
salt ☐
pepper ☐
food ☐
fish. ☐

7 All months have
years ☐
summers ☐
weeks ☐
days ☐
seasons ☐
Sundays. ☐

8 All schools have
desks ☐
students ☐
blackboards ☐
classes ☐
teachers ☐
gymnasiums. ☐

9 All houses have
garages ☐
windows ☐
gardens ☐
dining rooms ☐
kitchens ☐
stairs. ☐

10 All cities have
a post office ☐
streets ☐
roundabouts ☐
traffic lights ☐
shops ☐
crossroads. ☐

11 All bathrooms have
a bath ☐
a shower ☐
a toilet ☐
taps ☐
a mirror ☐
a bidet. ☐

b Compare your answers.

3 Read and think

a Read the following short story.

One day a woman was sitting in front of the mirror in her hotel room. She was putting on her make-up, getting ready to go out.

Suddenly there was a knock at the door. The woman went and opened it. There was a young man outside. He was tall, dark and very good-looking. When he saw her, he said, 'Oh, I'm sorry! I thought this was my room.' He then walked on down the corridor, towards the lift.

A few seconds later the woman phoned the reception desk and told them to stop the man. She said she was almost sure he was a thief.

b Why did the woman think the young man was a thief?

4 Listen to this

Look at the words below.

rubbish	fancy
reckon	starving
cross	pour
positive	strong

You may know what some of them mean. But all of these words have more than one meaning.

Listen to the short conversations, and then write down (in English!) what the words mean in each of them.

1 ....

2 ....

3 ....

4 ....

....

5 ....

6 ....

7 ....

5 Play games in English

Word pyramids

Form two teams. The teacher names a category or group of words, for example, numbers, countries, animals, drinks, school subjects, sports, clothes, furniture, etc.

In only one minute, each team has to make a pyramid with a one syllable word on top, a two syllable word under it and a three syllable word on the bottom.

Examples:

Numbers
one
seven
eleven

Animals
dog
monkey
elephant

6 Time to talk

Moments in your life

a Think for three minutes about:

the most embarrassing moment in your life.
the happiest moment in your life.
the worst moment in your life.
the most frightening thing which has ever happened to you.

b Form groups. Tell the rest of the group about the things you thought of. Did any of you have similar experiences?

7 Now you're here

Find out the answers to the following questions by asking a British person.

- Which is the:
  second biggest city in Britain?
  oldest university?
  longest river?
  highest mountain?
  most popular daily newspaper?
  most popular Sunday newspaper?
  most popular television channel?
  most popular television programme?
  most popular radio channel (Radio 1, Radio 2, Radio 3, or Radio 4)?
- Who is the most popular/ unpopular member of the Royal Family?
- Who is the youngest member of the Royal Family?
- What is the most beautiful part of Britain?
- Which is the ugliest city?
- What is the most popular pet?
- Which is usually the warmest/ (coldest) month in Britain?
- Which is the most common boy's/ girl's name?
- What is the most common name for a pub?
- Which is the most common word in the English language?

Compare your answers.

Strange but true

Have you ever read a story in a newspaper which you *can't* believe? These newspaper stories, believe it or not, are all true.

Seven shops in the town of Melton Mowbray have given a job to Mr Jack Beaver. His job? Every day he goes to each shop after they close, and jumps up and down on the rubbish in their dustbins.

"I've never had such an easy job," said Mr Beaver. "After I've done it just a few times, they can put twice as much rubbish in the next day!"

Mr Beaver weighs 120 kilos.

Mr Fred Diplock of Neasden, North London, is trying to sell his house. He hasn't had any luck yet.

"The garage has been the problem," said Mr Diplock yesterday. "I built it myself last year, but I made a small mistake. The garage is higher than the drive. You can get into the garage of course— I've built four steps up into it.

Quite a lot of people have already come to see the house. But nobody's bought it yet. I've told them that the garage is a very useful extra bedroom. But it's useless for a car, I'm afraid!"

Mrs Jane Wisty of Downend, Bristol, rang the police yesterday. "I've just seen a dead body!" she told them. "It was in the boot of a car. The boot was open and I could see two legs hanging out."

The police contacted all the police cars in the area.

"We've just had a report of a car with a dead body in it," one police car reported. "We've seen it too. We're following it now."

A few minutes later the police stopped the car. The 'dead body' got out of the boot. It was a car mechanic.

The driver of the car explained, "I've had a funny noise from the back of my car for a long time. The mechanic just wanted to find out where it came from."

The police have decided not to arrest the driver or the mechanic.

I Who said what?

Who do you think said these things? Write a, b, c, d or e in the boxes.

a) the police officer
b) Mrs Wisty
c) Mr Diplock
d) the mechanic
e) Mr Beaver

1 ☐ As you can see, I'm not dead.

2 ☐ Nine-nine-nine . . . Ah, officer, I've just seen something very strange . . .

3 ☐ It's a good thing I'm so heavy.

4 ☐ Did you know there's a dead body in your boot?

5 ☐ No, I'm afraid you can't use it for a car.

6 ☐ It was the only way to find out where the noise is coming from.

7 ☐ Nobody wants it— I don't know why!

8 ☐ It's good exercise. I've already lost 5 kilos!

2 Three interviews

Work in pairs.

a Interview Mr Beaver.

Have you got a job yet, Mr Beaver?

....

Who do you work for?

....

What do you do?

....

Is it a difficult job?

....

Why did they choose you for the job?

....

b Interview Mr Diplock.

Have you sold your house yet, Mr Diplock?

....

How many people have come to see the house?

....

Why haven't they bought it?

....

c Interview Mrs Wisty.

What did you see?

....

What did you do then?

....

What happened when the police stopped the car?

....

Have the police arrested the driver or the mechanic?

....

3 What's just happened?

a 📼 Work in groups. Listen to the sound effects on the cassette.

b Discuss them and then decide what has just happened.

Example:
He's just seen a ghost.

4 Think of answers

Work in pairs. Think of answers to these questions.

Why are you	crying? angry? smiling? so tired? laughing? frightened?

Because I've . . .

Example:
Why are you so happy?
Because I've just had a letter from my boyfriend.

5 The things you've done (or not done)

a Write down three things you haven't done yet in Britain but which you want to do before you leave.

Example:
I haven't been to London yet.

b Write down three things you've never done in your life but want to do.

Example:
I've never windsurfed.

c Write three things you've done but which you never want to do again.

Example:
I've eaten fish and chips!

d Compare your sentences in groups.

6 Quick questions

Find as many students as you can in only 3 minutes who have:

swum in the English Channel
been to a British police station
gone out with an English boy/girl
eaten an Indian take-away
seen *Eastenders* on television
spoken in English on the phone
sent more than five postcards
broken something in their host family's house.

The 'winner' is the student with the most names.

Grammar summary: page 86

49

1 Travelling by train

A *Can I have a ticket to <u>London</u>, please?*
B *Single or return?*
A *Return, please.*
B *Are you coming back today?*
A *Oh yes, this evening.*
B *So you want a cheap day return then. That's £11.97 . . . Thank you.*
A *What time does the next train leave, please?*
B *At <u>10.24</u>.*
A *And what time does it get to <u>London</u>?*
B *At <u>11.52</u>.*
A *Which platform does it go from?*
B *Platform <u>3</u>.*
A *Do I have to change?*
B *No, it's a through train.*
A *Thanks very much.*

a Practise the dialogue in pairs.

b Change roles. Change the underlined words/numbers.

Example:
Canterbury
£8.56
16.32
17.40
5

2 How to get there by Underground

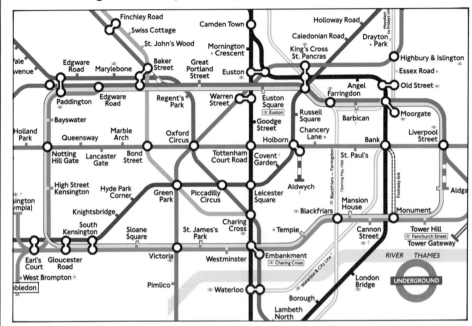

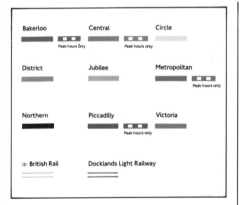

Look at the map. In pairs, work out the best way to make the following journeys.

From Bond Street to South Kensington
From Marble Arch to Victoria
From Tottenham Court Road to Westminster
From Waterloo to Notting Hill Gate

Example:
From Piccadilly Circus to St Paul's

- Take the Bakerloo Line, northbound.
- Get off at Oxford Circus.
- Change to the Central Line, eastbound.
- Get off at St Paul's.

3 Travelling by bus

A *Does this bus go to <u>Marble Arch</u>, please?*
B *<u>Marble Arch</u>? No, you want the <u>89</u>. There's one every <u>ten</u> minutes.*

(ten minutes later)

C *Hold very tight now . . . Fares, please.*
A *<u>Marble Arch</u>, please.*
C *<u>60p</u>, please.*
A *Thanks. And can you tell me where to get off, please?*
C *<u>Marble Arch</u>? OK. Fares, please. Any more fares?*

Work in pairs. Change the underlined words to other places in London and other fares. Change roles.

4 Travelling by taxi

A ACE Taxis.
B Can you send a taxi to 10, Milton Road, please?
A What's your name, please?
B Michelle Leduc.
A Can you spell that?
B L-E-D-U-C.
A And where do you want to go?
B To the station.
A Right, it'll be there in about ten minutes.
B Good. Thank you.

(10 minutes later)

C Taxi for Leduc.
B OK, I'm coming.
C To the station, isn't it?
B Yes, that's right.

(15 minutes later)

C Here we are.
B How much is that, please?
C £4.55
B Thank you. Keep the change.

Practise the dialogue in pairs. Use your own names and addresses. Change roles.

5 Travelling by coach

Coaches are long-distance buses. They travel between all the big cities in Britain. They are quite fast, comfortable and cheap. Many coaches now have toilets and hostesses who serve drinks and snacks.

Work in pairs. Student A reads the instructions below. Student B reads the instructions on page 80.

You want to go to Cambridge. Ask student B questions to get the information you need. He/She will ask you for information about a trip to Bournemouth.

		To Cambridge	To Bournemouth
1	Cost of a day-return ticket	....	£12.95
2	Time of the first coach you can catch	....	06.30
3	Time the coach arrives	....	10.05
4	Bay	....	3
5	Time of the last coach back	....	19.00

6 What's missing?

Listen to the short telephone conversations on the cassette and fill in the missing information in the table.

	Taxi company	Taxi to	Name of passenger	Address	Telephone number
1					
2					
3					

Summary of English in situations

● using public transport

1 🔊 Sound right

a Listen to these words and underline the stressed syllables.

Example: <u>pro</u>blem

seven	evening
prison	information
student	arrive
afraid	automatic
umbrella	machine
letter	escalator
company	station
answer	address

b Listen again and circle the *unstressed* syllables with the sound [ə] in them.

Example: probl(em)

c Now listen and repeat the words. Make sure you put as *much* stress as possible on the stressed syllables and as *little* stress as possible on the syllables with [ə] in them.

d Now use as many of the words in a) as you can in one sentence.

Example:
There are seven automatic escalators at the station.

2 🔊 Listen to this

a Listen to a girl speaking on the telephone to a boy.

b Now listen to some questions on the cassette. Tick the correct answers below.

	Yes	No			Yes	No
1	☐	☐		6	☐	☐
2	☐	☐		7	☐	☐
3	☐	☐		8	☐	☐
4	☐	☐		9	☐	☐
5	☐	☐				

c Now listen to the conversation again. This time you can hear what Peter says. Check your answers.

3 Work on words

Which things on the left do you usually keep in the 'containers' on the right? Match words from the two boxes.

Example:
cup – coffee

rubbish	bookcase
wine	vase
spare tyre	bucket
clothes	packet
bird	**cup**
jam	cupboard
car	bottle
sardines	briefcase
money	envelope
crisps	dustbin
plates	car boot
books	cage
water	box
letter	wardrobe
coffee	garage
matches	jar
documents	tin
flowers	wallet

4 Play games in English

Word families

a Form teams. The teacher says a word and each team writes it in the middle of a blank sheet of paper.

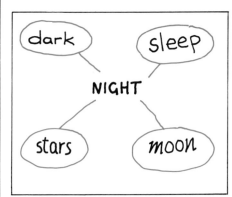

b In only two minutes, each team writes down as many words as they can think of associated with the first word.

The team with the most words is the winner.

5 Read and think

a Read the following information carefully.

- Mark is taller than Andrea.
- Tim is a student.
- David is taller than Sarah.
- Tim is shorter than David.
- Sarah has got a job.
- Sarah is shorter than Mark.
- Andrea is going out with David.
- Andrea isn't shorter than Tim.
- Sarah is shorter than Tim.
- Mark isn't taller than David.
- David doesn't like Sarah.

b Now answer these questions:

1 Who is the tallest of the five?
2 Who is the shortest?
3 Who is taller—Mark or Tim?

6 Time to talk

Just a minute

a Form two teams. The teacher gives both teams 'a subject'.

Examples:
this town	British food
Saturdays	my brother / sister
rock music	the school I go to
football	

b Students have three minutes to think of what to say on that subject.

c The teacher chooses a student who must try to talk for one minute without stopping. The student gets one point for the team if he / she talks for half a minute and two points if he / she talks for a whole minute. If the student stops talking, a student from the other team takes over the subject.

7 Now you're here

Find out the answers to the following questions.
- At what age must you pay full fare on:
  the buses in this town?
  British Rail?
- Can you hire a bicycle in this town / area? (If so, where?)
- How much does a cheap day-return ticket by train to Central London cost?
- Is it cheaper to go by coach or bus?
- When can you catch a train if you've got a cheap day-return ticket?
- What time does the last train leave London for your town?
- What is the speed limit for cars:
  in towns?
  on motorways?
- What is a BritRail Pass?
- How much does an eight-day pass cost?
- Can you buy them for longer periods?
- Can you get a Youth Pass?
- How much does a return ticket by coach to Oxford or Cambridge cost?
- Is there a video / a hostess / a toilet on the coach?
- Can you buy a ticket on the coach?
- What is the name and telephone number of a local taxi company?
- What do taxis charge extra for?

GRAMMAR IN ACTION

As others see us

Every year millions of visitors come to Britain. What do they think of the country and the people?

A French girl outside Buckingham Palace said:
"I'm so excited. I've just seen the Queen! She came out in a Rolls Royce. I've been interested in your royal family since I was a little girl. I've read all the stories — especially about Charles and Diana — in French newspapers and magazines. They tell me what your royal family really do. Your newspapers can't tell the truth about them!"

An Italian boy, who was in Britain for the first time, talked about the weather.
"I can't understand it. I've been here for over a week, and I still haven't seen any fog!"

A Japanese student from Tokyo said:
"I've been in Britain since April, and I'm living with a British family. I've noticed one big difference between British and Japanese families. British men do jobs like cooking, washing up and ironing. They're jobs which I've never seen Japanese men do. They think it's women's work. But I don't agree!"

A German student, at a language school in Oxford said:
"I thought Britain was a modern European country — you've been in the EEC for years now. So why do you still use miles, pints, and pounds, instead of kilometres, litres and kilos? And why do you still drive on the wrong side of the road?"

A Danish girl who works as an au pair in Brighton said:
"I came to Britain a month ago. I've noticed one very strange thing here. After British people have washed the dishes, they never rinse them. They just take them out of the dirty, soapy water and leave them to dry!"

A Swedish girl said:
"I've watched a lot of television since I arrived in Torquay two weeks ago. British television's brilliant! But the 'programmes' which I've enjoyed most are the advertisements. They're very funny or very clever, or both. Back home in Sweden we don't have any TV advertisements at all!"

1 Who said what?

Who do you think said these things?
Write a), b), c), or d) in the boxes.

a) Italian boy   d) Danish girl
b) Japanese boy   e) French girl
c) German girl   f) Swedish girl

1 ☐ It makes shopping very difficult. For example, I don't know what size shoes or jeans to ask for.

2 ☐ Did you know that he's not speaking to her at the moment, except in public?

3 ☐ I enjoy guessing what they're for, you know beer or toothpaste or whatever, before they actually name the product.

4 ☐ I help too— my friends at home would be very surprised if they could see me.

5 ☐ In fact the sun hasn't stopped shining—it's not at all like in old films and Dickens's novels.

6 ☐ Surely it's not difficult to put them under the cold tap for a moment?

2 Make true sentences

The Italian boy		(have)	in Britain since April.
The Japanese boy		(be)	a lot of TV.
The German girl		(notice)	stories about the Royal Family.
		(read)	problems with British measurements.
The Danish girl	has (n't)	(watch)	that British people don't rinse dishes.
			any fog yet.
The French girl		(see)	the Queen.
The Swedish girl			

3 For or since?

a Write sentences about the pictures using the verbs and *for* or *since*.

Example:
(be) in prison
1960.
*He has been
in prison for
29 years —
since 1960.*

1 (have)
January

2 (live)
70 years

3 (know)
1975

I speak English very well

4 (study)
10 years

5 (be married)
50 years

6 (wear glasses)
1970

b Work in pairs. Ask and answer questions about each picture.

Example:
A *How long has he been in prison?*
B *For 29 years.* or *Since 1960.*

4 What about you?

Ask each other in pairs.

1 How long have you been in Britain?
2 How many pages of this book have you done?
3 How many excursions have you been on?
4 How much money have you spent on clothes?
5 How many records/cassettes have you bought?
6 How much money have you spent on books/newspapers/magazines?
7 How many different sports have you played?
8 How many times have you been to the cinema/a disco?
9 How many British people have you got to know well?
10 Have you changed your mind about British people since you came here?

5 What's the word?

a Form two teams. Prepare questions about jobs, machines, shops, etc.

Examples:
What do you call a person who repairs cars? (a mechanic)
What do you call a machine which cleans carpets? (a hoover/vacuum cleaner)
What do you call a shop which sells newspapers? (a newsagent's)

b Each team asks the other team their questions, one at a time. A correct answer scores one point.

Grammar summary: page 86

1 Asking permission

A *Excuse me, Barbara, can I ask you something?*
B *Yes, what is it?*
A *Well, some of us are going to Shades disco tonight. Is it all right if I stay out a little later?*
B *How much later?*
A *Until one o'clock maybe.*
B *One o'clock! No, that's far too late!*
A *But it doesn't start until nine thirty.*
B *Well, I think a couple of hours is enough. Not later than midnight, please.*
A *OK, I'll try not to be late, but you know how few buses there are at that time.*
B *Well, if you leave the disco at 11.30, you shouldn't have any problems.*
A *Could I have a front door key, please?*
B *No, I'll wait up for you.*

a Practise the dialogue in pairs. Change roles.

b Imagine you are in the situations opposite. Make up your own dialogues using these phrases.

Is it all right if I . . . ?	Yes, of course. Yes, all right.
Is it OK if I . . . ?	Yes, sure.
Can I . . . ?	No, I'm sorry . . .
Could I . . . ?	No, I'm afraid not
May I . . . ?	(+ excuse)

1

2

3

4

5

C Act out your dialogues in pairs. Change roles.

2 Invitations and offers

A *Do you want to dance?*
B *Yes, OK.*

A *Would you like to sit down?*
B *Yes, good idea.*

A *Would you like a drink?*
B *Yes, please.*

a Practise the dialogues in pairs.

b Student A invites B, using the words below.

Example: walk
A *Would you like to go for a walk?*
B *Yes, OK / good idea!*

walk	tennis
cinema	cup of coffee
disco	shopping
beach	drink
McDonald's	pizza

C Change roles.

3 Invitations and excuses

🔊 Listen to the conversation between Nick and Cindy and then answer the questions.

1 What is Nick's telephone number?
2 What is Cindy doing tonight?
3 Fill in the missing information.

	Cindy's invitation	Nick's excuse
This evening		tired, going to bed early
Tomorrow		
Friday		
Saturday		

4 Making excuses

Work in pairs. Student A wants to go out with student B, but B doesn't want to go out with him/her. B makes excuses using the pictures below, and his/her own ideas.

Start your excuses with phrases like this:
No I'm sorry, I'm . . . ing.
No, I'm afraid I must . . .

Example:
A *Would you like to come out with me tonight?*
B *No, I'm sorry. I'm going to bed early.*
A *What about tomorrow then?*
B *No, . . .*

2

3

1

4

5 Role play

Work in pairs. Student A reads the information below. Student B looks at the information on page 81.

Situation 1

You want to go to the cinema with student B. It's a horror film. It starts at 8.00. Phone B and invite him/her. Try to persuade him/her to come with you.

You can use phrases like these:
Why don't you want to?
Oh, come on!
Are you sure?

Situation 2

Student B phones you and invites you to play tennis. You're not very good at tennis, and you haven't got a tennis racket.

Summary of English in situations
• asking permission • inviting and making offers • accepting/refusing invitations and offers • apologizing and making excuses

1 ☒ Sound right

a Listen to these phrases and sentences.

take a bus
a cup of tea
black or white?
bread and jam
I'm from Spain.
What's the time?
He's ill in bed.
Where do you live?
Come at ten to ten.
Mark can dance but he can't sing.

b Listen again and put a circle around the unstressed words like this:

(a) cup (of) tea

c Listen and repeat the phrases and sentences. Try to say the unstressed words as quickly and as lightly as you can. Notice that these words are usually unstressed:
a   an   the
do   does   can
of   at   from
or   but   and

d Think of some phrases or sentences of your own and mark the unstressed words.

2 Listen to this

☒ Listen to these people talking. They're all travelling. Which form of transport are they using? Choose from the ones in the pictures below.

1	4 ....
2	5 ....
3	6 ....

3 Work on words

Match the words on the left with the pictures on the right to make short sentences.

Example: I a
You post a letter.

1 post
2 feed
3 try on
4 press
5 cash
6 fill in
7 dial
8 switch on
9 lock
10 pack
11 catch
12 brush
13 play
14 ride
15 read

4 Play games in English

Glug

One student (student A) thinks of a verb. The other students in the class try to guess the verb by asking questions which contain the invented regular verb 'to glug'.

Example:
Student B *Is it easy to glug?*
Student A *Yes, quite easy.*
Student C *Can you glug?*
Student A *Yes, I can.*
Student D *When do you glug?*
Student A *Usually in the summer.*
Student E *Did you glug last night?*
Student A *No, I didn't.*
Student F *Are you glugging now?*
Student A *No, I'm not.*
Student G *Where do you usually glug?*
Student A *In the sea.*
Student H *Is the verb 'swim'?*
Student A *Yes, it is.*

Student H then thinks of another verb. The class can only ask twelve questions and have only one guess.

5 Time to talk

Whose job?

a Work in groups. Make a list of jobs around the house.

Examples:
shopping for food
cleaning the car
washing up
cooking
putting up shelves
clearing the table
doing the ironing

b Each student puts the jobs in one or both of these columns.

Women's jobs	Men's jobs
	shopping for food

c Compare your lists in your groups and discuss the differences.

6 Now you're here

Radio and television

Find out the answers to these questions by asking a British person.

- What sort of programmes do they have on BBC Radio 1?
  Radio 2?
  Radio 3?
  Radio 4?
- What are the names of the local radio stations in your town/area? (Which ones are commercial stations?)
- What are the names of the four television channels?
- What, if any, are the differences between the sort of programmes the television channels show? Where does the BBC get its money from?
- How much does a TV licence cost for a) a black and white TV? b) a colour TV?
- How many times an hour do they have commercial breaks on ITV?

GRAMMAR IN ACTION

A funny thing happened . . .

A man had a grandfather clock. The clock wasn't working properly, so he decided to take it to a clock repairer. As he was walking down the street, he turned a corner and bumped into a woman who was coming the other way.

"You stupid man!" she said angrily, as she was getting up. "Why can't you wear a watch like other people?"

A man came into a pub. He had a bandage over one ear. A friend of his was standing at the bar.

"What happened? What's the matter with your ear?" he said.

"I burned it."

"How did you burn it?" his friend said curiously.

"Somebody telephoned while I was ironing."

A girl was watching a film in a cinema. Her dog was sitting quietly in a seat next to her. The manager of the cinema saw the dog and said angrily to the girl,

"You mustn't bring your dog in here." So the girl took the dog out. As they were walking out, the girl said to the manager,

"It's a pity. He was really enjoying the film."

"I'm surprised," said the manager sarcastically.

"Yes, so am I," said the girl. "He didn't like the book at all."

1 Make true sentences

Make sentences by matching the text in the two columns. Put the verbs in brackets into the correct tenses (past continuous or past simple).

Example:
The woman (come) round the corner when she (bump) into the man with the clock.
The woman was coming round the corner when she bumped into the man with the clock.

1 The girl and her dog (watch) a film
2 The man with the clock (walk) down the street
3 A man (stand) at the bar
4 The dog (enjoy) the film
5 The man with the bandage (iron)

a) when he (bump) into a woman.
b) when the manager (speak) to the girl.
c) when the telephone (ring).
d) when the man with the bandage (come) in.
e) when the manager (see) it.

2 What happened?

Describe what was happening in the pictures opposite when something else suddenly happened. Use the verbs below each picture in your sentences.

Example:
drive   stop
While she was driving home, a police car stopped her.
or
A police car stopped her while she was driving home.

1 watch   sit

2 sleep   come

3 lie   steal

4 talk   arrive

5 play   shoot

3 Find out

Find a person in the class who:

- was having breakfast at seven o'clock this morning
- was having a bath at ten o'clock yesterday evening
- was shopping at three o'clock yesterday afternoon
- was watching a film on television at midnight last Saturday
- was still sleeping at ten o'clock last Sunday morning.

The first person to find five people is the winner.

4 What were they doing?

a Send a student (A) out of the room.

b The other students in the class must all do something, either together or in pairs. Choose from the verbs below.

talk	write	smile	hide
draw	eat	sleep	dance
read	clap	cry	look for

c Start to do the things you have decided on. Student A comes back into the room. He / She looks at what everybody is doing for 30 seconds. Then they all stop.

d Students ask student A, in turn:
What was I doing when you came into the room?
or
What were we doing . . . ?

Student A answers:
You were reading, etc.

5 How do they speak?

Listen to some conversations on the cassette. Write down *how* people were speaking to each other. Choose from the words below.

excitedly angrily quietly slowly sarcastically loudly nervously

1 ....
2 ....
3 ....
4 ....
5 ....
6 ....
7 ....

6 What about you?

a Write answers to the following questions. You can write as much as you like.

What do you do | quickly?
well?
badly?
slowly?
noisily?
carefully?

b Work in pairs. Ask each other the questions.

Example:
A *What do you do quickly?*
B *I eat quickly.*

Grammar summary: page 86

1 Parts of the body

a Choose the words from the box to label the parts of the body.

arm	shoulder	chest	stomach	leg	knee		foot/feet
neck	wrist	ankle	head	ear	back	nose	finger
mouth	throat	tongue	eye	tooth/teeth		toes	hand

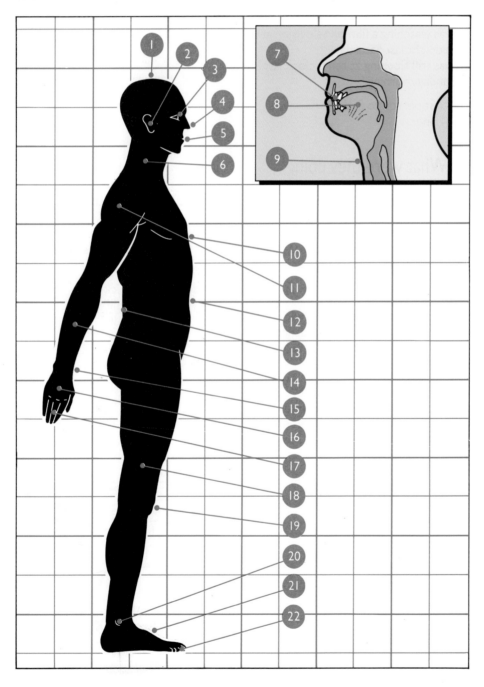

b Work in pairs. Student A points to a part of his/her body. Student B says what it is in English. Change roles.

2 Feeling ill

A *What's the matter? You don't look very well.*

B *I don't feel very well. I've got a <u>headache</u> and a <u>sore throat</u>.*

A *<u>Why don't you go to the doctor's?</u>*

B *Yes, that's a good idea.*

A *Shall I make an appointment for you?*

B *Yes, please.*

a Practise this dialogue in pairs. Change roles.

b Now change the underlined words. Choose from the ones below.

I've got	a stomach ache.
	earache.
	a temperature.
	a (bad) cold.
	a cough.
	flu.
	a pain in my back.

You'd better	take an aspirin.
You should	go to bed.
	lie down.
	take some medicine.

c Change roles. This time choose from these words and phrases:

						ill.
	arm					awful.
	leg					terrible.
My	shoulder	hurts.	I feel			dizzy.
	back					sick.

You'd better	take an aspirin.
You should	go to bed.
	lie down.
	take some medicine.

62

3 What's the matter?

a One student comes to the front of the class. The teacher writes down on a card (or whispers) what is wrong with him/her. The class ask the student, 'What's the matter?' The student mimes what is wrong and the class try to guess. The student who is miming must not talk.

Example:
You feel sick and you've got a headache.

b If the class guess correctly, they must give the student advice.

Example:
You should take an aspirin/go to bed.

4 At the doctor's

A *Sit down, please, Miss Vernier. What's the problem?*
B *I've got a headache and a sore throat and I feel terrible!*
A *I see. Can you open your mouth, please? Say 'Ah'.*
B *Ahhhh!*
A *Yes, you've got flu, I'm afraid. I'll give you something for it.*

(pause)

A *Here's a prescription for some tablets.*
B *What do I do with this? I don't understand.*
A *Take it to a chemist's, and they'll give you the tablets.*
B *Do I have to pay?*
A *Yes, but not very much. Take the tablets three times a day after meals. And you'd better stay in bed for a couple of days.*
B *Thank you, Doctor, goodbye.*

a Practise the dialogue in pairs. Change roles.

b Now practise the conversation with other students, without looking in the book. Student B (the patient) can change his/her problem.

Student A (the doctor) can change his/her advice. Use your own ideas.

5 What's the problem?

Listen to this conversation and fill in the missing information in the doctor's notes.

Problem?

How long for?

Cause?

Prescription for?

How many?

How often?

When/come back?

If you're ill in Britain

If you are from an EC (European Community) country or from one of these countries—Austria, Norway, Sweden, Yugoslavia (and some others), you can see a doctor, or ask him to visit you, or go to hospital, free. If a doctor gives you a prescription, you get the medicine from a chemist's and pay for it there.
If you are not from one of the above countries you can still get emergency treatment free.

Summary of English in situations

- talking about parts of the body
- asking/saying what's the matter
- at the doctor's

1 Sound right

	day [eɪ]	my [aɪ]	care [eə]	now [aʊ]

a Find the words which have the same sounds—[eɪ], [aɪ], [eə], or [aʊ]. Put them in the right columns above.

name	out	buy	make
square	great	rain	town
house	wear	right	ice
white	chair	there	mouth

b 📺 Work in pairs. Say the words in each column to each other.

c Work in teams. Think of other words to go in each column. The team with the most correct words is the winner.

2 Play games in English

What are they like?

Form two teams. The teacher writes a short sentence on the board with an adjective missing. Team A then complete the sentence with an adjective beginning with A, team B with a word beginning with B, etc.

Example:
Teacher *My father's a . . . man.*
Team A *My father's an angry man.*
Team B *My father's a boring man.*
Team A *My father's a clever man.*

If one team can't think of a word in ten seconds, the other team win a point. The teacher then starts a new round with a different sentence.

3 Work on words

a Work in teams. Put the words in the box into ten groups.

Example:
banana apple pear orange

shoes	fridge
butter	cake
church	carrots
banana	wheels
knee	yoghurt
hospital	trousers
onions	biscuit
pear	orange
jumper	cheese
elbow	ankle
trainers	bread
apple	slippers
tights	cooker
engine	library
milk	sprouts
school	dishwasher
shoulder	brakes
cabbage	washing machine
doughnut	skirt
boots	steering wheel

b Now think of other words which go with the words in each group.

Examples:
banana apple pear orange
cherry plum

4 Time to talk

Break their alibi

Last night some thieves broke into the language school where you are studying and stole a large sum of money. Two students are suspected. The police are going to interview them.

a The teacher chooses two students (a boy and a girl). They leave the room and prepare an alibi for last night (from 7 o'clock till midnight).

b The rest of the class is divided into two groups of detectives (A and B). They spend five minutes preparing questions like these:

Where did you go last night?
Where did you have dinner?
What was your friend wearing?
Who paid for the meal?

c The two suspects come back in. One is interviewed by the detectives in group A, the other by the detectives in group B.

d After five minutes, the two suspects change places. The detectives ask the same questions to both suspects and note down any differences in their stories.

If there are more than two differences, the suspects are guilty.

5 Listen to this

Listen to the jokes on the cassette and match each joke with the correct picture below.

a) ....

b) ....

c) ....

d) ....

e) ....

f) ....

6 Read and think

Work in pairs or groups.

Only *one* of these statements is true. Which one?
Write your answer—don't shout it out!

1 Only one of these statements is false, the others are all true.
2 Only two of these statements are false, the others are all true.
3 Three of these statements are true, five are false.
4 Half the statements are true, half are false.
5 All of these statements are false.
6 All of these statements are false, except one.
7 None of these statements is true.
8 All of these statements are true.

7 Now you're here

Abbreviations

a Ask a British person what the following abbreviations mean.

1	Mon.	13	hrs
2	in.	14	incl.
3	lb.	15	ft
4	dept	16	yd
5	info.	17	Xmas
6	prog.	18	cm.
7	tel.	19	cont.
8	Co. Ltd.	20	doz.
9	etc.	21	ctd
10	no.	22	max.
11	Oct.	23	yr
12	Rd	24	Dr

b Make a list of other abbreviations you see, and try to find out what they mean. Look especially at the small advertisements in shop windows and in local newspapers.

UNIT ELEVEN
LESSON ONE

WIMBLEDON
FACTS AND FIGURES

For fifty weeks of the year, Wimbledon is a quiet suburb in south-west London. But every summer, for the last week in June and the first week in July, it is the centre of the world — at least it is for anyone who is interested in tennis.

These are just a few facts about the Wimbledon championships.

- The tournament was first played at Wimbledon in 1878.

- 21,600 balls are used during the championships. Yellow balls were first used in 1986.

- 103 ball boys and ball girls are chosen from local schools. They start training early in May. Among other things, they are taught to stand or kneel absolutely still while the players are playing. They mustn't even chew gum or scratch their noses.

- The 650 matches are controlled by 330 umpires and line judges. They are all given strict eye tests (although some players don't believe it!). This test is important because the ball from a service often hits the ground at over 150 k.p.h.

- Umpires are not allowed to leave their chairs during a match, even to go to the toilet!

- Line judges are changed every two hours because it's a tiring job. On one famous occasion a line judge fell asleep in front of millions of television viewers. She was later sacked from her job!

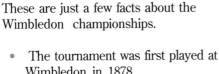

- Wimbledon is famous for its strawberries and cream. Every year, about 275,000 portions of strawberries are eaten by spectators during the fortnight. The cream is poured onto the strawberries by a team of eighty people.

- When the centre court was built, they forgot to build an exit for the enormous roller. It's still there today!

- The centre court is only opened 24 hours before the tournament starts. The rest of the year it is closed.

1 Make true sentences

1 The tournament	is	changed every two hours.
2 21,600 balls		used during the championship.
3 Line judges		first used in 1986.
4 Ball boys and ball girls	are	given eye tests.
5 Umpires and judges		chosen from local schools.
6 The matches		first played in 1878.
7 The centre court	was	eaten by the spectators.
8 275,000 portions of strawberries	were	only used during the Wimbledon fortnight.
9 Yellow balls		controlled by 330 umpires and line judges.

2 Where were they made?

a Make a list of things that you've got or that you're wearing.

Examples:
a radio   a calculator   a sweater
trainers   a camera   a watch
perfume   jeans

b Work in pairs. Ask each other questions like this:

A *Where was your watch made?*
B *It was made in Switzerland.*

3 Who was it?

a Write three things which happened to you yesterday, on a piece of paper. They must all begin, 'I was . . .'

You can use the verbs in the box if you want to.

ask	send	give	meet	stop
choose	drive	tell	leave	teach
beat	pay	help	take	
wake	show	lend	call	

Examples:
I was woken by my alarm clock at 7 o'clock.
I was given a lift to school by my host.
I was asked out by an English boy.

b Put the piece of paper into a hat or bag. Take out a different piece of paper, and read the sentences to the class like this:

X was woken by his / her alarm clock at 7 o'clock.
etc.

c The rest of the class guess who wrote the sentences.

4 What else?

Form two teams. The teacher says a word (a noun), for example, 'English'.

Team A start by saying a sentence:
        English is spoken.
Team B *English is written.*
Team A *English is read.*
Team B *English is learned.*

The game goes on like this until one team can't think of another verb, or they make a mistake.
The teacher then says another noun, and so on.

5 Newspaper headlines

a Work in pairs or small groups. Expand the headlines into complete sentences. Use your imagination.

10 HURT IN MOTORWAY CRASH

Example:
Ten people were hurt in a crash on the M1 motorway yesterday afternoon.

GIRL SHOT IN BANK RAID

Liverpool beaten 3-0 by United

Woman murdered in London flat

POP STAR GIVEN 6 MONTHS TO LIVE

Diamonds stolen from millionaire's home

KIDNAPPERS PAID £1 MILLION

PICASSO PAINTING SOLD FOR £5 MILLION

b Now think of the next two lines of the newspaper reports.

Example:
The accident happened as a lorry was passing a coach full of American tourists. The coach hit the lorry and then . . .

c Read out your sentences in class.

Grammar summary: page 87

Rules of the house

① You must be on time for meals.

② You must come home before 11 o'clock.

③ You mustn't use the telephone without permission.

④ You mustn't have friends in your room.

⑤ You can't smoke in your room.

⑥ You can't have a bath without permission.

⑦ You are not allowed to play loud music in your room.

⑧ You are not allowed to take food or drink from the fridge without asking.

1 The rules of your house

Tick (√) those rules above which are true in your family in Britain or in your family at home.

2 Can you or can't you?

Ask another student questions like these about the rules.

Can you come late for meals?   Yes, I can. / No, I can't.
Do you have to come home before 11 o'clock?   Yes, I do. / No, I don't.
Are you allowed to smoke in your room?   Yes, I am. / No, I'm not.

Make notes of his/her answers. Then tell the rest of the class about the rules in his/her house.

3 Different families, different rules

Listen to these foreign students talking about their English families. Mark the things they are allowed to do with a tick (√) and the things they are not allowed to do with a cross (×).

	Come home late?	Smoke in his/her room?	Have a bath every day?	Have friends in his/her room?
Pedro				
Chieko				
Rosa				
Helmut				

4 Role play

Work in pairs. Act out the conversations in these situations.

1

2

3

4

5 What are they doing wrong?

Many of the people in this picture are doing something wrong. Find the people and make sentences.

Examples:
You're not allowed to walk on the grass.
You mustn't drop litter.
You must drive on the left.

6 What do the signs mean?

What do these signs or symbols mean?

Example:

You	're not allowed to	turn right.
	mustn't	

Summary of English in situations

- talking about rules and obligations

1 Sound right

a 📷 Listen and underline the stressed words.

Example:
What's the time?

You can't come to school by car.
Can you pass the salt, please?
I don't want it.
What did he do?
Would you like to come?
I want to talk to you.
We don't know his name or his age.
I've got two French girls in my class.
I'm not sure, but I think so.

b Now practise saying the sentences with the stress on the right words. Try to say the unstressed words as quickly as you can.

c The words which carry the important information are stressed. Make a list of them. What sort of words are they?

Example:
It's a *hot day*.   hot = adjective
                     day = noun

2 Listen to this

📷 Listen to some short conversations, and make notes as you listen. At the end you must answer two questions.

1 How much does the boy spend during the evening?
2 How much does he have left at the end of the evening?

3 Time to talk

Professional tennis players can earn thousands of pounds a year—sometimes millions of pounds.

a Look at this list of jobs. Put them in order according to:

how much you think people in your country earn for these jobs.
how much you think they *should* earn.

a secondary school teacher
a nurse
an army captain
a police officer
a fire fighter
a refuse collector
a politician (Member of Parliament)
a lawyer
a hairdresser
an airline pilot
a prison guard
a pop singer
a priest
a car salesperson

b Discuss your answers in pairs or groups. Do you agree? Explain why you put the jobs in that order. Use the words below if you want to.

dangerous	useful	difficult
easy	necessary	exciting
enjoyable	important	boring
responsible	dirty	interesting

Try to convince each other you are right.

4 Work on words

Put the following words in the right order.

Example:
extra large medium large small
small medium large extra large
or
extra large large medium small

1 freezing warm cold hot
2 good terrible bad fantastic
3 teenager child adult baby
4 worse best worst better
5 yesterday today
  the day before yesterday
  tomorrow
6 afternoon morning evening
  night
7 yard mile inch foot
8 month day week year
9 white dark grey black
  light grey
10 love like hate dislike
11 fourth second first third
12 half third quarter three-
  quarters
13 tonight tomorrow evening
  last night tomorrow night
14 ninety nine nineteen ninety-
  nine
15 minute second hour day
16 village city town country
17 lane path motorway road
18 twenty past eight half past eight
  quarter to eight twenty to eight
19 autumn summer spring
  winter
20 gram kilo ounce pound

5 Read and think

Read through these two problems, and try to solve them. Write your answers, and then compare them with those of other students.

1 A boy and his father were driving on a motorway when they had a terrible accident. The father was killed, and the boy was badly injured. He was taken to hospital in an ambulance. He was still unconscious when a doctor came to examine him. 'Oh no!' the doctor cried out. 'It's my son!' How was this possible?

2 There were six glasses on the bar, three full and three empty. The barman bet me £5 that I couldn't rearrange them so there would be one full, one empty, one full, etc. He told me I was only allowed to move one glass. How did I win the bet?

6 Play games in English

Read my thoughts

Form two teams. One student from each team (A and B) sits at the front of the class.
The teacher writes half a sentence on the board, for example:

If it rains tomorrow . . .

Every student in the class then writes a complete sentence.

Examples:
. . . I'll stay at home.
. . . we'll get wet.
. . . I won't go out.

Student A then reads out his/her complete sentence. His/her team gets one point for each team member who has written the same sentence. The idea is for each team to predict what A and B have written.

7 Now you're here

What do they mean?

The following slang words or idioms are common in spoken English.

1 a kid
2 a mate
3 a fag/a ciggie
4 to nick
5 ta
6 cheers
7 a quid
8 to chat someone up
9 to fancy someone
10 a fiver
11 a bloke
12 a yob
13 weird
14 a rip off
15 to be shattered

a Ask a British person what they mean.

b What other slang words or idioms have you heard?

71

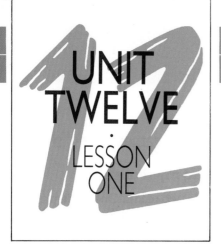

1 What's it been like?

a Write short answers to these questions.

b Compare your answers in groups.

1 When did you come to Britain?

2 How did you come to Britain?

3 How long did the journey take?

4 What surprised you most when you arrived?

5 How much English did you understand when you first arrived?

6 How much English do you understand now?

7 Have you been staying with a British family?

8 What's different about British houses/flats compared to houses/flats in your country?

9 What's the food been like?

10 Which food did you like most/least?

11 Who did you speak English to most?

12 Have you spoken to many British people of your own age?

13 Which television programmes have you watched?

14 Which newspapers or magazines have you read?

15 Which sports have you played?

16 What sort of things have you done in the evening?

17 What has the weather been like?

18 Which excursion/trip did you like most?

19 Where else did you go?

20 Is Britain more or less expensive than your own country?

21 Which things are more expensive?

22 Which things are cheaper?

23 How much money have you spent?

24 What did you spend it on?

25 Have you bought any clothes/presents/souvenirs?

26 When are you going to leave Britain?

27 What are you going to miss?

2 Noughts and crosses

a Form two teams: noughts (0) and crosses (X). One team (0) choose a word from the first box below and make a sentence with that word. If the sentence is correct, they cross out the word and put an 0 in the square. If the sentence is wrong, they don't do anything. Then team X have a turn. The winner is the first team with a line of noughts or crosses (horizontally, vertically or diagonally).

b The teams go on to the second and third sets of boxes.

often	much	doesn't
this	do	some
hotter	many	those

worse	since	were
for	ago	angrily
will	best	ever

got	did	who
which	any	went
gone	yet	didn't

3 Do you remember?

a Form two teams. Write at least fifteen questions about the lesson 1 texts and stories in this book.

Examples:
What do you wear if you want to keep warm when you're windsurfing?
What does a dentist give you if you've got a hole in a tooth?
What did Chris order in the cafe?

b Take it in turns to ask each other the questions.

28 Would you like to come back? Why?

29 Are you going to write to anybody after you get home?

30 What's the strangest thing you've noticed about Britain and British people?

31 In what ways have your opinions of Britain and the British people changed?

32 What has been the most embarrassing/worst/most enjoyable experience since you arrived?

1 Saying goodbye

A *You'd better hurry!*
B *It's OK. I'm ready now.*
A *Have you got everything?*
B *Yes. I think so. Just a minute . . .
    passport, money, ticket . . . Yes, I
    think that's all.*
A *Good. Well, I hope you've enjoyed
    yourself.*
B *Yes, I really have. And thank you very
    much for everything. I've had a great
    time.*
A *Good, I'm glad. Don't forget to write
    to us.*
B *No, I won't, I promise.*
A *Have a good journey, and give our
    regards to your family.*
B *Yes, I will. And thank you for looking
    after me so well. Goodbye!*
A *Bye.*

Practise the dialogue in pairs. Change
roles.

2 Who says what?

a) Take care!
b) Thank you for everything!
c) Give my regards to your family!
d) I've really enjoyed myself!
e) Are you sure you've got
    everything?
f) Thank you for looking after me!
g) Will you miss me?
h) See you again soon, I hope!
i) Have a good journey!
j) Don't forget to write!

a Work in pairs. Look at the pictures and the phrases in the box. Decide which is
the 'best' phrase for the speech bubble in each picture. You can use each phrase
only once.

1

2

3

4

5

6

b Compare your answers and vote which is the best phrase for each picture.

3 What's missing?

Look at the pictures. What does the other person say in each picture?

1

2

3

4

5

6

7

8

4 A quiz

Form two teams. The teacher asks the following questions alternately to each team.

What do you say if . . .

1 you're in a cafe and you want a cup of coffee with no milk or sugar in it?
2 you want to dance with somebody you don't know?
3 someone steps on your foot when you're dancing (He/She says sorry.)?
4 you're in a shop and you like a pair of jeans, but you don't know if they're big enough?
5 you want to speak to Paul on the phone?
6 somebody phones to speak to your friend Carol, but she's not in?
7 you've just finished eating, you're not hungry any more but you're offered a second helping?
8 your friend's looking ill?
9 somebody invites you to a party but you don't want to go?
10 you're in the street and you can't find the Post Office?
11 you're at a railway ticket office and you want to go to London and back?
12 you're in somebody's room and you want to smoke?
13 somebody asks you what date it is today?
14 you're leaving the British family you've been staying with?

1 Act it out

a Divide the class into groups of 3–4 students.

b Each member of a group chooses two of the phrases below.

c In no more than ten minutes, the groups should work out a short sketch containing the 6–8 phrases they have chosen.

d The groups act out their sketches in front of the rest of the class.

Choose from these phrases:

Would you like to dance?
Don't worry.
I haven't got any money.
Don't be silly!
You're welcome.
Here you are.
Great!
I can't—I'm busy.
Where were you?
Yes OK, good idea.
Why don't we go to the beach?
Yes, please.
What time can you be ready?
I'm very worried.
Can I help you?
It's too big.
Is it OK if I borrow your bike?
At half past nine, I think.
I'm sorry!
No thanks, I'm full.
What are you going to do?
See you tomorrow!
What's she like?
What a pity!
Is that really true?
Can I take a message?
I'm afraid I can't help you.
Who's speaking, please?
What's the matter?
No thanks, I'm too tired.
No, I don't think so.
How much are these?
What size are you?
Can I have a key, please?
In the morning usually.
Let me do it for you.

2 UK quiz

a Divide the class into two teams, A and B.

b Team A answer question 1, team B question 2, etc. If one team can't answer a question, the other team try to answer it.

Questions

1 What are the Severn, the Tyne, and the Avon?
a) mountains
b) lakes
c) rivers

2 Where does the British Prime Minister live?
a) 10 Downing Street
b) Buckingham Palace
c) Windsor Castle

3 Who invaded England after the Battle of Hastings in 1066?
a) the Vikings
b) the Romans
c) the French

4 What is Wembley best known for?
a) horse racing
b) football
c) rugby

5 It's 0° Centigrade. What is the temperature in Fahrenheit?
a) 32°
b) 50°
c) 15°

6 What is VAT?
a) a kind of tip
b) a sales tax
c) a motorists' organization

7 How many players are there in a cricket team?
a) 15
b) 8
c) 11

8 Which of these cities is in the Midlands?
a) Birmingham
b) Belfast
c) Brighton

9 What are the Tories?
a) Scottish mountains
b) the Conservative party
c) an English football team

10 What is the population of Britain?
a) 55 million
b) 45 million
c) 65 million

11 What are Paddington, Victoria and King's Cross?
a) airports
b) railway stations
c) ports

12 What are Dorset, Sussex and Devon?
a) towns
b) cities
c) counties

13 What is the capital of Eire (the Republic of Ireland)?
a) Belfast
b) Dublin
c) Cardiff

14 Who lived in Stratford-Upon-Avon?
a) Winston Churchill
b) Queen Elizabeth I
c) William Shakespeare

15 What are Spurs, Arsenal and QPR?
a) shops
b) football teams
c) political parties

16 What number do you dial if you want the police?
a) 000
b) 999
c) 111

17 What is the Princess of Wales' eldest son called?
a) William
b) Harry
c) Edward

18 How many sides has a 50p coin got?
a) 5
b) 6
c) 7

19 What sort of programmes can you listen to on Radio 1?
   a) pop music
   b) news and talks
   c) classical music

20 What are the Sun, the Guardian and the Independent?
   a) newspapers
   b) magazines
   c) cinemas

21 What are Harrods, Debenhams and Selfridges?
   a) shoe shops
   b) department stores
   c) chemists'

22 What are the Derby, the Grand National and the Gold Cup?
   a) rugby matches
   b) sailing races
   c) horse races

23 What are bitter, mild and lager?
   a) kinds of coffee
   b) kinds of beer
   c) kinds of chocolate

24 What is usually the wettest month of the year in Britain?
   a) January
   b) April
   c) July

25 Where would you go if you wanted to rent a flat?
   a) an off-licence
   b) an estate agent's
   c) a building society

26 What does the letter 'L' on a car mean?
   a) licence applied for
   b) low speed
   c) learner driver

27 What do double yellow lines mean?
   a) no waiting
   b) no parking 9 a.m. – 5 p.m.
   c) no parking at any time

28 Where do people speak Cockney?
   a) Cardiff
   b) London
   c) Birmingham

Unit 3 Lesson 1 Exercise 4
(page 19)

a Work in pairs. Student A reads the information about Tim on page 19. Student B reads the information about Helen below.

b Student A asks student B questions about Helen and fills in the missing information about her.

Examples:
How many hours a week does she watch television?
What time does she get up?

c Student B ask student A the same questions about Tim and fills in the missing information about him.

Helen	*Tim*
Watches TV:	
10 hours a week	....
Gets up:	
7.45	....
Has a bath/shower:	
every day	....
Has a steady boyfriend:	
no	....
Goes to the cinema:	
once a month	....
Brushes her teeth:	
three times a day	....
Smokes:	
five cigarettes a day	....
Goes to church:	
never	....
Sleeps:	
8 hours a night	....

Unit 3 Lesson 2 Exercise 4 (page 21)

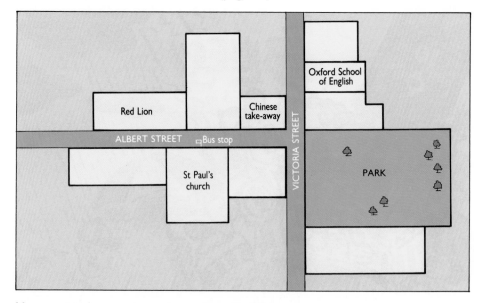

You want to know where these places/buildings are:
1 the post office
2 the Midland Bank
3 the Cannon cinema
4 the chemist's
5 the record shop
6 the sports centre

Find and mark them on your map with the information you get from student A.

Take it in turns to ask and answer questions. (Student A starts.)
Ask each other questions like this:
B *Excuse me. Where's the post office, please?*
A *It's . . . .*

Unit 4 Lesson 1 Exercise 4
(page 25)

Work in pairs. Student A is Chris and reads the instructions on page 25. Student B is Andrea and reads the instructions below.

You are Andrea. It's a year later. You're working in the same cafe again. Chris comes in but you don't recognize him at first. When he says who he is, explain why you didn't reply to his letter. Tell him what you thought of him a year ago. Decide if you want to go out with him now.

Unit 4 Lesson 1 Exercise 6 (page 25)

This is Andy's room later in the day, when he gets back. He notices that ten things are different, proving that someone has been in his room.

a In your teams, make a list of the things which are different or missing.

Examples:
There was a coffee cup on the table. Now it's on the floor.

There were four cassettes on the shelf. Now there are only two.

b Now test each other in pairs. Student A looks at the two pictures and tests student B with questions like these:

How many cassettes were there in picture 1?
How many cassettes are there now?
Where was the coffee cup in picture 1?
Where is it now?

Change roles after three minutes. Who answered the most questions correctly?

Unit 4 Lesson 2 Exercise 5 (page 26)

Work in pairs. Student A reads the information on page 26. Student B reads the information below.

Look at the information about these two people. Student A will ask you questions about them.

Name: Sophie Pierce
Address: 76 Quantock Road
          Taunton
          Somerset
          TN14 SKL

Name: Stephen Chamberlain
Address: 68 Sycamore Crescent
          Marlborough
          Wiltshire
          SN48 5GL

Now ask student A questions about these two people and fill in the missing information about them. Ask A to spell any difficult words.

Name: ....
Address: ....
....

Name: ....
Address: ....
....

Unit 6 Lesson 2 Exercise 5
(page 39)

Work in pairs. Student A reads the instructions on page 39. Student B reads the instructions below.

You are a shop assistant. You've only got three jumpers left in your sale:

red   size 34   £14.99
green   size 38   £13.99
light blue   size 36   £15.99

Talk to the customer and try to persuade him/her to buy a jumper. Be very friendly.

Unit 7 Lesson 2 Exercise 4 (page 44)

Work in pairs. Student A reads the instructions on page 44. Student B reads the instructions below.

```
Dale T.C, 89 Church Rd,Sandford On Thames ....... Oxford 774387
Dale T.C, 9 Maple Rd ............................. Bicester 253898
Dale T.C, 5 White Wy ............................. Kidlington 71528
Dale T.J, 22 Morton Clo .......................... Kidlington 2946
Dale W.F, 48 High St ............................. Kidlington 4883
Dale Windows, Unit 2 Fitzharris Trading Est ...... Abingdon 30237
Dale W.M, The Flat 5 St. Leonards Ct .........
Dale-Emberton R.A, 13 Kings Orchard,
                   Brightwell-cum-Sotwell ..Wallingford 33640
Dale-Green C.J, 58 Butler Clo ....................Oxford 53390
Dales,International Road Haulage,Twyford ........Banbury 811441
Dales Cash Stores Ltd, High St ................... Didcot 812221
Dales G.A, 13 Sunnyside,Hollow Wy ........ Oxford 779045
Dales R, 20 Flatford Pl .......................... Kidlington 79114
Dales R, 47 Selwyn Cres,Radley .............. Abingdon 27908
D'Alessandro C.Talbot, 4 Squitchey La .............. Oxford 58467
Daley A.B, Downham Cott,Asthall ................. Burford 3413
Daley B, 25 Spruce Rd ............................ Kidlington 6311
Daley C.J, 29 Witan Wy ........................... Wantage 4372
Daley J.J, 1 Belvedere Rd,Cowley ............ Oxford 725735
Daley M.S, 48 Witan Wy ........................... Wantage 4457
Daley P.A, Stanton Ho .............. Stanton St. John 807
Daley R.D, 5 Childrey Wy,E Challow .............
Daley R.M,
         Manor Cott,Horton-cum-Studley ..Stanton St. John 442
Daley S.J, 2 Flatford Pl ......................... Kidlington 6961
Daley T, 23 Abbotts Clo .......................... Didcot 812555
Daley W, Snowdrop Ldge,Mill La .............. Upper Heyford 2304
Dalgarno J.A, 14 Otwell Clo ...................... Abingdon 32804
DALGETY AGRICULTURE Ltd,Agric Mrcnt,
                               Edward St ..Banbury 4477
Dalgleish C.J, 11 Thames Mead ............ Wallingford 37061
Dalgleish M,
         Foxcombe Rse,Foxcombe Dv,Boars Hill ..Oxford 730330
Dalgleish T, 380 Marston Rd ......................
Dalitz R.H, 28 Jack Straws La,Headington ..........Oxford 62531
D'All S.J, 22 Richens Dv ......................... Carterton 843457
Dallaire R, Kennel Cott .......................... Nettlebed 641925
Dallal E.S, 12 Masefield Cres,Tithe Fm .......... Abingdon 25697
Dallas A, 92 Fernhill Rd,Begbroke ................Kidlington 4272
Dallas Brett,Solrs—
         25 Beaumont St ......................... Oxford 513557
Dallas Brett,Solrs, 25 Beaumont St ................ Oxford 513557
Dallas C, 75 Iffley Rd ........................... Oxford 721479
Dallas Keith Chemical & Eng Ltd,
         Bromag Indust Est,Burford Rd,Minster Lovell ..Witney 73061
Dallas Keith Ltd,
         Bromag Indust Est,Burford Rd,Minster Lovell ..Witney 73061
Dallas Management Services Ltd, 8 South Pde ...... Oxford 514142

Daly Rev Eltin, 18 Leopold St ..................... Oxford 240325
Daly E.T, 55 Lark Down ......................... Wantage 68408
Daly H.A, 1 Park Cotts,Lower Greenfields,
                        Christmas Com ..Watlington 2046
Daly J, 19 Blenheim Gdns,Grove ................ Wantage 69843
Daly J, 12 Hill Rd .............................. Watlington 2556
Daly J, 21 Hillview ............................. Carterton 842839
Daly J.F,
         Corpus Christi Fm Ho,Sandford Rd,Littlemore ..Oxford 715156
Daly J.F, Corpus Christi Farm Ho,Sandford Rd,
                        Littlemore ..Oxford 773779
Daly K.J, 19 Abingdon Rd,Tubney ......... Frilford Heath 390882
Daly Michael, 7 Goodson Wlk ................. Oxford 724105
Daly M, 39 Marston St ........................... Oxford 728203
Daly M.J, 104 Lime Wlk...........................Oxford 68955
Daly M.P, 35 The Grates,Cowley ............ Oxford 771455
Daly N, 6 Blencowe Clo ......................... Bicester 243263
Daly Dr N.A, 93 Rose Hill ....................... Oxford 775445
Daly P.C, Maytree Cott,Astall ................. Burford 3571
Daly R, 115 Holloway,Cowley .................. Oxford 776814
Daly T, 80 Cherwell Rd,Berinsfield ........... Oxford 340973
Daly T, 40 The Firs ............................ Brill 238397
Daly T.G.C, 49 Hedgemead Av .............. Abingdon 27448
Daly V.C, 1,Clearfield Cott,Wotton ........... Brill 237050
Dalziel W, 7 Barbary Dv,Grove ............... Wantage 67494
Dalziel A, 27 Francis Little Dv ............... Abingdon 32291
Dalziel Keith, 25 Hampden Dv ................ Kidlington 2623
Dalziel M.S, 368 Woodstock Rd ...............
Dalziel S, 29 Tweed Cres ...................... Bicester 244901
Dalziel T.W, 6 Hampden Rd ................... Wantage 67504
Daman P.J, Church Cott,Shilton ............... Carterton 842072
Damerell C, 4 Godfrey Clo ..................... Abingdon 23418
D'amico M, 141 Corn St ........................ Witney 72869
Damjanovic L, 301 Cowley Rd .................. Oxford 725429
Damm F, 11 Grange Pk .......................... Steeple Aston 47269
Dammarell L.M, 49a Queens Rd ................ Carterton 845066
Damms B.J, 7 Park End .........................
Damnjanovic M, 22 Fieldside,Upton ............. Blewbury 850991
Damnjanovic P, 40 Mowbray Rd ............... Didcot 816273
Damp Guard & Timbertech, 45 West St,Osney ...... Oxford 241648
Dampa Ltd,Acoustic Ceiling Mfrs,
         Wimblestraw Rd,Berinsfield ..Oxford 340471
Dampa Marine Ltd, Wimblestraw Rd,Berinsfield ... Oxford 340842
DAMPCURE-WOODCURE /30,Damp,Timb Treatment—
Branches,
         30 Wendover Rd ........................Aylesbury 85411
Dampness Analysis Ltd,Bldg Dampness Conslt,
         Friars Cott,Market Sq ..Princes Risboro 3535
```

Find out the missing telephone numbers from student A.

Ask questions like this:

What's W.M. Dale's phone number?

Unit 8 Lesson 2 Exercise 5
(Page 51)

Work in pairs. Student A reads the instructions on page 51. Student B reads the instructions below.

You want to go to Bournemouth. Ask student A questions to get the information you need. He/she will ask you about a trip to Cambridge.

	To Bournemouth	To Cambridge
1 Cost of a day-return ticket	....	£8.95
2 Time of the first coach you can catch	....	07.00
3 Time the coach arrives	....	08.20
4 Bay	....	7
5 Time of the last coach back	....	20.05

Unit 9 Lesson 2 Exercise 5
(page 57)

Work in pairs. Student A reads the
instructions on page 57. Work in
pairs. Student B reads the instructions
below.

Situation 1

Student A phones you to invite you
out. You don't want to go out with
him/her. Make excuses but be
friendly.

Situation 2

Phone student A and invite him/her
to play tennis.
You've got two tennis rackets.
Try to persuade A to play with you.

Use phrases like these:

Why don't you want to?
Oh, come on!
Are you sure?

GRAMMAR SUMMARY

Unit I

to be **(present tense)**

Affirmative	
I am	(I'm)
you are	(you're)
he is	(he's)
she is	(she's)
it is	(it's)
we are	(we're)
you are	(you're)
they are	(they're)

Negative	
I am not	I'm not
you are not	you aren't / you're not
he is not	he isn't / he's not
she is not	she isn't / she's not
it is not	it isn't / it's not
we are not	we aren't / we're not
you are not	you aren't / you're not
they are not	they aren't / they're not

Questions
Am I . . . ?
Are you . . . ?
Is he . . . ?
Is she . . . ?
Is it . . . ?
Are we . . . ?
Are you . . . ?
Are they . . . ?

to have got **(present tense)**

Affirmative		
I	have (I've)	got . . .
You	have (You've)	got . . .
He	has (He's)	got . . .
She	has (She's)	got . . .
It	has (It's)	got . . .
We	have (We've)	got . . .
You	have (You've)	got . . .
They	have (They've)	got . . .

Negative
I haven't got . . .
You haven't got . . .
He hasn't got . . .
She hasn't got . . .
It hasn't got . . .
We haven't got . . .
You haven't got . . .
They haven't got . . .

Questions
Have I got . . . ?
Have you got . . . ?
Has he got . . . ?
Has she got . . . ?
Has it got . . . ?
Have we got . . . ?
Have you got . . . ?
Have they got . . . ?

The present simple tense

Affirmative		
I	want	
You	want	
He	wants	
She	wants	a drink.
It	wants	
We	want	
You	want	
They	want	

Negative			
I	do not	(don't)	
You	do not	(don't)	
He	does not	(doesn't)	want a
She	does not	(doesn't)	drink.
It	does not	(doesn't)	
We	do not	(don't)	
You	do not	(don't)	
They	do not	(don't)	

Questions		
Do	I	
Do	you	
Does	he	
Does	she	want a
Does	it	drink?
Do	we	
Do	you	
Do	they	

Short answers
Yes, I do. / No, I don't.
Yes, you do. / No, you don't.
Yes, he does. / No, he doesn't.
Yes, she does. / No, she doesn't.
Yes, it does. / No, it doesn't.
Yes, we do. / No, we don't.
Yes, you do. / No, you don't.
Yes, they do. / No, they don't.

can **(present tense)**

Affirmative		
I	can	
You	can	
He	can	
She	can	speak English.
It	can	
We	can	
You	can	
They	can	

Negative	
I cannot (can't)	
You cannot (can't)	
He cannot (can't)	
She cannot (can't)	speak English.
It cannot (can't)	
We cannot (can't)	
You cannot (can't)	
They cannot (can't)	

Questions	
Can I	
Can you	
Can he	
Can she	speak English?
Can it	
Can we	
Can you	
Can they	

Unit 2

Present continuous (progressive) tense

Use the present continuous when you talk about what is happening *now*, at this moment.

Example:
I'm falling!

Affirmative		
I	am (I'm)	
You	are (You're)	
He	is (He's)	
She	is (She's)	falling.
It	is (It's)	
We	are (We're)	
You	are (You're)	
They	are (They're)	

Negative	
I'm not	
You aren't / You're not	
He isn't / He's not	
She isn't / She's not	falling.
It isn't / It's not	
We aren't / We're not	
You aren't / You're not	
They aren't / They're not	

Questions	
Am I	
Are you	
Is he	
Is she	falling?
Is it	
Are we	
Are you	
Are they	

Imperatives

Examples:
Concentrate. (Affirmative)
Don't worry. (Negative)

Demonstratives

This (singular)
These (plural) } here / near you

That (singular)
Those (plural) } there / not near you

Unit 3

There is / There are

Singular	Plural
There } is ... isn't ...	There } are ... aren't ...
Is there ...?	Are there ...?

Countable nouns

- Positive sentences: *a lot of*

  Example:
  A lot of teenagers watch TV.

- Negative sentences: *(not) many*

  Example:
  Not many teenagers smoke.

- Questions: *many*

  Example:
  How many fillings have you got?

Uncountable nouns

- Positive sentences: *a lot of*

  Example:
  They need a lot of sleep.

- Negative sentences: *(not) much*

  Example:
  They don't get much pocket money.

- Questions: *much*

  Example:
  How much time have we got?

Unit 4

to be **(past simple)**

Affirmative	
I	was
You	were
He	was
She	was
It	was
We	were
You	were
They	were

Negative		
I	was not	(wasn't)
You	were not	(weren't)
He	was not	(wasn't)
She	was not	(wasn't)
It	was not	(wasn't)
We	were not	(weren't)
You	were not	(weren't)
They	were not	(weren't)

Questions
Was I?
Were you?
Was he?
Was she?
Was it?
Were we?
Were you?
Were they?

There was / There were

Singular	Plural
There was . . .	There were . . .
There wasn't . . .	There weren't . . .
Was there . . .?	Were there . . .?

The past simple tense: regular verbs

Affirmative	
I	
You	
He	
She	walked.
It	
We	
You	
They	

Negative	
I	
You	
He	
She	didn't walk.
It	
We	
You	
They	

Questions		
	I	
	you	
	he	
Did	she	walk?
	it	
	we	
	you	
	they	

Past simple tense: irregular verbs

Present	Past
have	had
find	found
send	sent
be	was / were
know	knew
come	came
get	got
sit	sat
give	gave
tell	told
make	made
put	put
see	saw
say	said
forget	forgot
write	wrote

Infinitive of purpose

Use the infinitive with *to* when you give the reason for something.

Example:
They came to Bournemouth to have a swim.

some **and** any

- Positive sentences: *some*

  Example:
  She gave him some jam.

- Negative sentences: *any*

  Example:
  There wasn't any jam.

- Questions: *any*

  Example:
  Have you got any jam?

Unit 5

Adverbs of frequency

Adverbs of frequency usually go before the main verb.

	always	
	usually	
I	often	wear a uniform.
	sometimes	
	hardly ever	
	never	

Adverbs of frequency go after the verb *to be*.

	always	
	usually	
I'm	often	late.
	sometimes	
	hardly ever	
	never	

Comparatives of adjectives

- Add *– er* to short adjectives.

  Example: *strict*
  Rules were stricter.

- Put the word *more* before long adjective

  Example: *traditional*
  Subjects were more traditional.

Irregular comparatives

good	better
bad	worse

Ordinal numbers

1st	first
2nd	second
3rd	third
4th	fourth
5th	fifth
6th	sixth
7th	seventh
8th	eighth
9th	ninth
10th	tenth
11th	eleventh
12th	twelfth
13th	thirteenth
14th	fourteenth
15th	fifteenth
16th	sixteenth
17th	seventeenth
18th	eighteenth
19th	nineteenth
20th	twentieth
21st	twenty-first
22nd	twenty-second
23rd	twenty-third
24th	twenty-fourth
30th	thirtieth
31st	thirty-first

Months   Days

Months	Days
January	Monday
February	Tuesday
March	Wednesday
April	Thursday
May	Friday
June	Saturday
July	Sunday
August	
September	
October	
November	
December	

Unit 6

The future tense: going to

Affirmative

I am	(I'm)	
You are	(You're)	
He is	(He's)	
She is	(She's)	going to leave.
It is	(It's)	
We are	(We're)	
You are	(You're)	
They are	(They're)	

Negative

I am not	I'm not	
You are not	You aren't / You're not	
He is not	He isn't / He's not	
She is not	She isn't / She's not	going to leave.
It is not	It isn't / It's not	
We are not	We aren't / We're not	
You are not	You aren't / You're not	
They are not	They aren't / They're not	

Questions

Am I	
Are you	
Is he	
Is she	going to leave?
Is it	
Are we	
Are you	
Are they	

love / hate / enjoy / (don't) like + gerund

| I | love / hate / enjoy / don't like / like | dancing. |

Unit 7

First conditional

Use *if* + the present simple to talk about things in the future which can happen or which are possible. Then use the future with *will* for the result. In other words, 'If A happens, B will happen.'

Example:
If you go to England, you'll learn a lot of English.

Superlatives of adjectives

- Add −*est* to short adjectives.

  Example: *short*
  The shortest queue.

- Put *the most* before long adjectives.

  Example: *expensive*
  The most expensive shoes.

Irregular superlatives

good	the best
bad	the worst

GRAMMAR SUMMARY

Unit 8

The present perfect tense

Affirmative		
I You	have	
He She It	has	decided.
We You They	have	

Negative		
I You	have not (haven't)	
He She It	has not (hasn't)	decided.
We You They	have not (haven't)	

Questions		
Have	I you	
Has	he she it	decided?
Have	we you they	

Unit 9

The present perfect with for and since

- Use *for* with periods (lengths of time).

  Examples: *for* | *five minutes*
  two days
  thirty years

  'for . . . . . .' answers the question 'How long?'

- Use *since* with times, dates, etc.

  Examples: *since* | *two o'clock*
  last Friday
  1987

Present perfect v past simple

Use the present perfect:

- about things which happened in the past but which still have an effect in the present.

  Example:
  I've lost my key.

- with *just, yet, already, never* and *ever*

- with *for* and *since*

Use the past simple:

- about things which happened in the past and are finished now, usually with words and phrases which indicate exactly when something happened.

  Example:
  I lost my key | *yesterday.*
  last month.
  two days ago.

Relative pronouns who, which

Use *who* when you talk about people.

Example:
A Danish girl who works as an au-pair in Brighton said . . .

Use *which* when you talk about things and animals.

Example:
The programmes which I've enjoyed most are the advertisements.

Unit 10

The past continuous tense

Affirmative		
I	was	
You	were	
He	was	
She	was	eating.
It	was	
We	were	
You	were	
They	were	

Negative		
I	was not	(wasn't)
You	were not	(weren't)
He	was not	(wasn't)
She	was not	(wasn't)	eating.
It	was not	(wasn't)
We	were not	(weren't)
You	were not	(weren't)
They	were not	(weren't)

Questions		
Was I		
Were you		
Was he		
Was she		eating?
Was it		
Were we		
Were you		
Were they		